THE NEMESIS EFFECT

Michael Shotter

ISBN-13: 979-8465880121

The following is a work of fiction.
Any similarities to any real-world persons, places, or events
are purely coincidental.

CHAPTER 1

THE POD

Tom Hallett was accustomed to keeping his eyes closed as he moved through the world. Like everyone else around him, he had been provided with ocular and cerebral implants upon reaching adulthood that allowed him to view information about his surroundings, which was automatically layered over his normal vision in an advanced form of augmented reality. Street names, weather statistics and forecasts, news and stock tickers, indeed, virtually any fragment or mass of data he might require in any given moment was available to him with a simple thought.

Of course, like those around him, Tom had quickly learned the value of being able to turn off all of that, either to focus on a particular source of information, or to relish the calm, soothing darkness that could still be achieved if one simply closed their eyes and cleared their mind.

As such, Hallett sat motionless, his eyelids sealed, as the pod, a sleekly-designed, autonomous vehicle he was riding in with a handful of strangers, made its way through an area of the city he preferred to ignore. In truth, the other passengers in the conveyance weren't total strangers to him, having seen at least a few of them previously in similar circumstances. After all, they each made regular use of the pod system and therefore possessed a vague awareness of one another as frequent passengers who'd shared the vehicle, or one effectively identical to it, enough times for that to occur. Still, these weren't people Tom was genuinely familiar with or attached to in any meaningful way. Of all of them, a particularly-well-dressed, somewhat-older woman, who he casually thought of as "the pretty lady" every time he'd encountered her, was the only one who'd managed to occupy any significant portion of his conscious mind for any length of time during his commutes.

Indeed, the "pretty lady" was present, revealed by the faint scent of her equally-attractive perfume circulating through the enclosed air of the pod. Hallett supposed that she was ultimately noteworthy to him not simply by virtue of her admittedly-compelling and obvious esthetic attributes but because she had an almost formal, refined air about her, as if she had either spent time in or aspired to join the executive class. It of course wasn't shocking to encounter such a person mingled with everyday citizens. To be sure, there were individuals who simply enjoyed presenting themselves in a more formal and elaborate manner of dress despite lacking an "executive" designation but Tom had to admit, there was something unique about her. "Perhaps it's her smile," he thought, summoning an image of her and studying it with his eyes still closed despite the woman literally sitting feet away from him. Conventional wisdom told him that this was a completely appropriate behavior, having been taught from a young age that it was impolite to stare, particularly when such an action was technically unnecessary.

The pod's electric motor whined a bit as it began to make its way up a slight gradient, which Hallett could have used to make himself aware of its precise location if the GPS transceiver in his implant weren't already able to do so on demand. They were traveling through the city's "old town," a cluster of homes that had been intentionally kept in the style of the late twentieth and early twenty-first centuries, its residents opting to forgo many of the esthetics and conveniences of modern life for a variety of reasons.

In Tom's mind, the whole idea of the place was a bit of an affront, an objective waste of land and resources that he felt could and should be better used to serve the needs of the city's current population, rather than catering to the whims of the comparatively-small group of citizens that lived within it. Still, as with many other things in life, Hallett had felt compelled to pick his battles when filling out his ballot in the most-recent election, using his limited number of votes to influence outcomes that had a more direct and meaningful impact on his own life. This was no doubt precisely as the refiners had intended when the new voting system had finally been instituted after decades of brutal, internal conflict that had taken the country to the brink of destruction on more than one occasion.

Tom had been a young boy when all that chaos had finally come to an end and had therefore become part of the first generation to meaningfully benefit from the outcomes and the renewed stability they brought. As ever, there were still isolated conflicts in the world at large but the US had managed if only by the slimmest of margins to defy the odds and persist far longer than most had thought possible when the homes around him had first been built.

It of course remained an imperfect system. There were still injustices, winners, and losers within the nation's borders but meaningful progress had been made, resulting in a populace that was generally better skilled, educated, and proactively inclined in most cases than could be said of their predecessors. Ultimately, that was the crux of Hallett's issue with "old towns," feeling as though they were an unnecessary concession to people who had effectively lost their bids to keep the world in the past, or who were simply unwilling or unable to move with it into the future and "get on board" with everyone else.

It was for these reasons that Tom had made a habit of keeping his eyes closed while traveling through old town despite it being a not-entirely-unattractive place. To be sure, it lacked the pristine, modern esthetics of the downtown area he was headed toward but it was far from a slum. Indeed, only telltale, occasional signs of trash, imperfect building facades, or items out of place that would have been automatically addressed by maintenance drones in any other part of the city revealed it to be a place that was kept up by people "when they got around to it."

As the pod reached the top of the hill, it unexpectedly slowed and Hallett opened his eyes, immediately realizing that something unusual was occurring. Pods did not generally stop in old town, its citizens either being unauthorized or unwilling to use them. Thus, when the machine's motor began to wind down, Tom had immediately felt compelled to scan the area for the passenger that was clearly about to board it.

Sure enough, Hallett quickly spotted a large man in a fine, dark suit exiting the front of an enormous, elaborate home and making his way along its sidewalk to the spot where the pod was about to come to a stop. For a moment, Tom wondered if the man might be a poser, a regular citizen who felt compelled to dress like an executive for a variety of reasons, but his implant quickly confirmed that he was the genuine article. Hallett's interest was piqued, noting that the approaching man was indeed a class three, indicated by the three gold stars that appeared to be projected from a small, round, black pin on his suit jacket's left lapel. There were dozens of executive classes, typically denoted by similarly-projected, elegant Roman numerals, but stars were reserved for the top three and most elite among them. Tom had of course seen class twos on various broadcasts as they often acted as representatives of the mega corporations they worked for but he had never even seen an image of a class one, or a class three in person before that moment.

At this realization, Hallett sensed the other passengers in the pod stirring and otherwise reacting as they became aware of the man and he immediately began to feel less awkward about being genuinely awestruck by what he was witnessing. Clearly, everyone in the pod was well aware of and equally-impressed by the significance of the development, which allowed Tom to confidently maintain his focus on the new arrival despite a vague realization that he was in fact impolitely staring at him.

The big man paused at the curb as the pod perfectly glided to a stop in front of him and the gull-wing door to the executive compartment at the front of the vehicle opened. The man, obviously noting the bewildered stares of the passengers in the pod's significantly-larger common area put up a hand and waved, giving them all a little nod and grin as he reached into the inner pocket of his suit jacket and retrieved a small pouch while stepping into his private chamber and taking his seat atop one of the two, luxurious positions that spanned nearly the full width of the pod.   There was a surge of excitement inside Hallett's mind as he felt certain if only for a moment that the man had specifically made eye contact with him. Objectively, he realized that this was highly unlikely and had no doubt that every other passenger in the pod felt precisely the same way but he nonetheless couldn't help feeling a little more special and important than he had a few moments prior, fully comprehending what a rare and noteworthy experience he was in the process of having. Class threes didn't simply walk around the world interacting with random, everyday people. These were individuals operating at such a high level and in positions of such power and authority that they almost seemed mythical to the average citizen. Thus, Tom's sense of exhilaration was compounded by the fact that he was now sitting just feet away from the man, a transparent, soundproof barrier and the back of the big man's seat the only thing separating them.

If he'd been able to pull his attention away from the new passenger, Hallett felt confident that he would have observed covetous looks of envy and outright jealousy for the position he currently occupied. He even imagined the pretty lady feeling compelled to move to the seat next to his, finding him suddenly more attractive and interesting by

4

proximity, but he wouldn't have noticed even if she had, thoroughly transfixed as he was on the man before him.

At any point, the big man could have activated the compartment's privacy mode, tinting the glass surrounding him and preventing himself from being observed, but he'd thus far chosen not to do that, allowing Tom to clearly and easily study him from behind.

Hallett imagined this was an intentional choice on the executive's part and was grateful for it, realizing that he likely would have quickly been reduced to an almost-pitiful state if he'd been denied the opportunity to make such observations. Tom therefore sat in rapt attention, carefully studying each move the big man made as he opened the little pouch he'd removed from his jacket.

Immediately, Hallett's mind ran through a series of exotic speculations regarding what the pouch might contain despite feeling confident that he would know for sure within moments. He felt almost giddy, understanding that every development he managed to observe would only add to the quality and veracity of the story he would no doubt tell for the rest of his life about the time he shared a pod with a class three executive.

Tom was therefore only slightly disappointed when the big man removed a handful of nuts from the package and began to eat them, one at a time, as the pod came back up to its normal cruising speed.

It was a mixed collection, consisting of several, small peanuts, a few walnuts, some almonds, and a single, large macadamia nut, which the executive had begun to methodically consume from smallest to largest in a manner that to Hallett seemed like a practiced ritual of sorts. As he did so, he stretched his long, thick legs out into the footwell of the compartment and Tom noted for the first time precisely how elaborate and impressive the man's shoes looked, with their polished, black finish perfectly reflecting all the little lights within the pod. "Truly," Hallett thought, "this is the most important man I'll likely ever encounter." That realization filled him anew with a mixture of excitement and sadness, both appreciating his good fortune but also reminding him that as a citizen, an archivist for the city's most-prominent news organization, he had effectively reached the pinnacle of his class and would never attain such a standing himself without transcending it, which was extremely unlikely to occur given his age and the circumstances of his life to that point.

As these thoughts played out and the big man steadily consumed the remaining nuts from his hand, a new thought began to slowly manifest in the archivist's mind. One of Tom's inherent gifts was an ability to draw connections between seemingly-unrelated events. It had been discovered via an aptitude test during his youth and had been fostered and encouraged, culminating in his profession as an adult. As such, his brain had almost immediately, subconsciously connected the dots of what was occurring around him in a way that few others could have but distracted as he was, the realization had come to him more slowly than it typically would have.

At the end of the block they were traveling along, there was an uneven bit of road where the human-maintained streets of old town transitioned back to the perfectly-smooth and predictable roadways of the rest of the city. It wasn't a huge bump by any means but it was significant enough that pod riders who regularly traveled through the area were well aware of it, consequently knowing to not be caught off guard or doing anything that might be negatively disrupted by it when it occurred.

Hallett was certain that the executive in front of him had no idea such a thing existed, further noting that the man would likely be finishing his nuts at precisely the time the transition would occur. Part of him firmly believed that this was a completely-inconsequential observation but as the pod approached the transition point, a nagging, more-substantial portion of his brain became increasingly convinced that something awful was about to happen to the executive in front of him. He tried to push the thought aside, realizing just how statistically unlikely what he was already envisioning was to occur. Still, the notion persisted and was exacerbated when the big man paused his consumption and briefly brought a hand up to his throat, apparently coughing slightly, before continuing at an even faster pace as if trying to make up for lost time.

As Tom watched the number of nuts in the executive's palm rapidly diminishing, he became completely convinced that the large macadamia would almost certainly enter the big man's mouth at precisely the moment of the inevitable bump. All at once, he was filled with an overwhelming compulsion to warn him of the impending event, regardless of his conscious mind's insistence that he was engaging in a ridiculous and paranoid line of thought.

A few seconds before the transition, Hallett sat, locked in a fierce internal debate between wanting to act and not wanting to appear foolish or unreasonable in the eyes of his fellow passengers, particularly the man in front of him. Finally, his potent, inherent concern for the well-being of others won out and he tapped his knuckles against the divider in an attempt to get the executive's attention but of course, the soundproofing was completely effective and the big man continued to eat, completely unaware of his effort.

A moment later, the class three executive casually tossed the whole macadamia into his mouth just as the pod hit the bump in the road, causing it to skip over his tongue and down into his throat where it became thoroughly lodged, blocking his windpipe. Immediately, the man's eyes bulged and he reflexively brought the hand that had been holding the nuts up to his chest in a fist, striking it in a vain attempt to dislodge the object. He then began rocking in his seat and kicking at the floor as he was quickly overwhelmed by an intense panic and the realization that he was unable to help himself.

The pod screeched to a stop and an alarm sounded in Tom's mind. This was a literal notification from his implant that had been specifically designed to get his immediate attention in the event of an emergency. That was followed by a slow, calm, synthetic voice in his head. "Tom Hallett," it began, confirming that the message was for him and therefore not being heard by the other passengers who were receiving their own, unique instructions. "Another passenger is having a medical emergency. You are the most qualified to provide assistance and are legally required to do so. Please exit the vehicle now!"

As the message began to replay in his mind, Tom saw the door of the executive compartment open in front of him as the big man began clawing his way toward it while the closest door to him did the same. For a moment, Hallett hesitated, not because he was unwilling to help but because he found it extremely unlikely the the limited first-aid training he'd received as a teenager and hadn't used since then made him the most qualified person present to respond to what had happened. He looked around at the other passengers, who each looked back at him with expectant stares, effectively communicating that they were both shocked by his lack of immediate action and simultaneously relieved that such action had not been demanded of them. The pretty lady in particular gave him an intense look that seemed to say, "Don't just sit there! Do something!"

Thus, Tom was spurred into action, getting up from his seat and making his way out of the pod, its door immediately closing behind him. To his left, the executive had also exited but the door to his compartment had remained open.

The big man staggered forward and hunched over before going to one knee and grabbing at his throat. In desperation, he turned to face Hallett and mouthed three words before collapsing to the ground. "Help me, please!"

Tom rushed over to the man, noting that his mouth had begun to make seemingly-involuntary gasping motions despite no sound or air passing through it as he lay front side down with his lower half on the sidewalk and his upper body in a patch of thick grass adjacent to it, his nearly-exhausted limbs barely quivering.

For a moment, Hallett was again stunned into inaction. He of course knew that the man before him was in need of the Heimlich maneuver but looking at his massive form, which no doubt weighed at least two hundred and fifty pounds, he was extremely doubtful that he could successfully lift him into position to administer it effectively, not having done any such thing in a very long time. As a teenager, Tom had pulled an older man out of a community swimming pool and given him mouth to mouth for a few moments before a medical drone had arrived when the man had suffered a rare, unpredicted heart attack but surely, that single incident hadn't qualified him for this, did it?

Conscious that he was in need of additional motivation, Hallett looked over toward the pod and once again saw the disturbed, seemingly-judgmental faces of his fellow passengers pressed up against the vehicle's windows in clear efforts to get the best-possible view of what was transpiring. Again, Tom made eye contact with the pretty lady and she nodded, urging him on with her eyes, which were beginning to water.

With that, Hallett reached down and rolled the big man over onto his back. His suit jacket had been left unbuttoned from when he'd first taken his seat and it immediately fell open at his sides, revealing his larger-than-expected gut and triggering a memory in Tom's mind of a variant of the Heimlich that could be performed on an individual in such a position. He reached down, pressing his palms into the bottom of the executive's belly, then shoved the mass down and up toward his chest.

At this, the big man's eyes widened anew and his extremities shook harder than ever as if purging themselves of their remaining energy. For a moment, his head came up off the ground slightly and tears began to roll out of his eyes, clearly still unable to breathe.

Above them, a pair of security drones swept into place and took up positions, having been recording the scene from their own unique angles as they'd approached.

The big man let out a smothered yet still chilling cry, using the last of his strength to reach up toward Hallett with his trembling, right hand as a few particles of salt from the nuts fell off of it, then collapsed back to the ground, completely exhausted.

"No!" Tom cried out, lifting himself back into position and bringing his hands down again with all his might, jamming the big man's gut up into his chest in a way that he would have felt completely uncomfortable doing under any other circumstance.

As the motion finished, the macadamia nut flew out of the executive's gaping mouth and arced through the space between them, striking Hallett in the forehead while the big man reflexively drew in a massive gulp of air and his body began shaking anew.

There was an enormous cheer from inside the pod as the other passengers erupted into a spontaneous, exuberant celebration and Tom rose back up in an effort to completely remove any pressure on the older man's body while he recovered. When his heaving began to subside, the executive looked up at Hallett with an expression of pure gratitude and mouthed three more words before passing out cold. "Thank you, sir!"

In Tom's head, the synthetic voice returned. "Thank you for your service to the community, Tom Hallett. Please immediately return the passenger to his compartment."

Instinctively comprehending that the man beneath him might well require additional medical attention despite his breathing having apparently returned to normal, Tom quickly bent down and hooked his arms under the big man's shoulders, then lifted his upper body off the ground slightly before beginning to drag him toward the pod's executive compartment. He briefly wondered if the voice in his head would have politely ordered him to do the same if the man had expired but decided that was a notion he preferred not to consider given how things had actually occurred. Indeed, Hallett felt amazing in that moment and far too good about the realization that he had literally saved a man's life to allow such a thought to linger in his exhilarated mind. Thus, when he reached the pod, he confidently and decisively lifted the older man's unconscious body up and into place atop his seat, high on adrenaline, then gently lowered him into what he hoped would be a reasonably-comfortable orientation spanning both of the available positions. Finally, Tom moved to the executive's feet, which were still dangling just outside of the pod's open doorway, noting the scuffs and marks that had appeared on the big man's shoes. In truth, they were still quite impressive, with their refined, clearly-bespoke design, but Hallett couldn't help noting that their distressed state seemed to somehow diminish the executive's overall appearance even more than the grass stains on his suit.

"Take care, sir," Tom said, gently lifting the man's feet and carefully placing them well inside the pod before standing and beginning to make his way toward his own entrance.

As soon as he was clear of it, the gull-wing door closed and the pod sped away, no doubt to the nearest hospital, leaving Hallett standing by the side of the road in a befuddled and admittedly slightly-vexed state. As he fully considered the validity of the pod's actions, the synthetic voice in his head returned. "A new pod has been dispatched to your location and your employer has been informed that your arrival will be delayed. Thank you again for your service to the community." With that, a timer appeared in Tom's augmented vision, indicating that it would be a little over two minutes before a new pod would arrive to collect and deliver him to his original destination.

Hallett grimaced a bit, realizing that the system had automatically done all of this in an effort to keep him on schedule for the day, which was simultaneously welcome and disappointing. On one hand, he often found himself appreciative of such conveniences, which he objectively knew helped to make his life easier and more efficient in a variety of ways. Still, having experienced such a monumental event in such a brief span of time, he couldn't help feeling that the system's relentless insistence to simply plow forward, making whatever adjustments it deemed necessary to see to such momentum without any consideration for that fact, felt uncomfortably cold and wrong in a way he wasn't accustomed to acknowledging. Indeed, for the first time, Tom felt himself potentially understanding why the residents of old town had made the choices they had, which rapidly became one of the most potent mental takeaways from his experience, much to his own shock.

With all these thoughts percolating in his mind, Hallett looked down and noted that the large, macadamia nut he'd extracted from the executive was still lying on the ground nearby. From down the street, he could see a maintenance drone approaching, no doubt on its way to tidy up the area and return it to its normal, pristine state. Realizing this, the archivist quickly bent down and picked up the nut, sliding it into his pocket and claiming it for himself as a souvenir of his unexpected adventure. Indeed, he would have a whopper of a story to tell for the rest of his days and a genuine piece of evidence to back it up.

In truth, the most important story of Tom Hallett's life had only just begun.

CHAPTER 2

CONSEQUENCES

Within minutes, Tom was back on the road in a new pod. Its passengers had briefly acknowledged his odd arrival, having been retrieved from a stretch of sidewalk with no obvious purpose beyond connecting two actual points of interest. Still, their attention had quickly reverted to their own interests and affairs, him being an ordinary citizen like the rest of them, with the only noteworthy thing about his appearance being the grass stains on the knees of his trousers.

As the pod plunged into the heart of the city, it quickly deposited the other riders at their destinations until Tom was the only one left inside it. A block later, the vehicle began to slow in front of the towering, regional headquarters of the media conglomerate that employed him and Tom readied himself to make his own exit.

To his surprise, the synthetic voice in his mind returned and delivered another message as the pod unexpectedly came back up to speed. "Tom Hallett, your presence has been requested by executive order. Your employer has been notified and your absence will not be penalized. Please, enjoy the ride, sir."

From the moment Tom had seen the macadamia nut come flying out of the executive's mouth and the color of life return to his face, a part of his brain had understood that something like this might happen. After all, he had unquestionably done something of consequence, a thing that he'd been feeling a significant amount of pride for even as he'd been preparing to enter his place of work and perform his typical chores for the day. Still, what he had done had been expected of him and indeed, would have been expected of any other passenger in his pod had they been tasked with it. Therefore, Hallett was genuinely surprised despite knowing that he was being taken to the hospital to likely receive a more formal "thank you" from the man he'd saved, or possibly his employer. The thought of that sent a chill up the archivist's spine. The idea of standing face to face with a class one, or even a class two, executive was something so foreign to him that it barely even seemed possible.

In a mercy to his swirling mind, the ride to the hospital was brief and Tom soon found himself inside it, making his way to the room number that had been indicated in his augmented vision when he'd exited the pod. "309," he thought, committing it to his natural, organic memory despite knowing such a thing was unnecessary. Every detail of his life was of course automatically stored in the cloud and could be retrieved at any time if forgotten but he nonetheless felt it important to note the number, seeing it as another vital detail of the expanding story he would someday tell.

As he reached the room, the door opened automatically and Tom stepped inside, knowing that it wouldn't have done so if he wasn't welcome and expected within it. In the hospital bed in front of him, the class three executive he'd encountered earlier nodded, making eye contact with him and waving him into the otherwise-empty room.

The big man was in a hospital gown, having been stripped of his clothing upon his arrival apart from the little, round lapel pin that had been transferred to the gown and continued to indicate his three-star status when observed through Tom's augmented vision. "Mr. Hallett," he began in a slightly scratchy but otherwise deep and potent voice, extending his right hand, which had been cleaned of any remaining salt by the hospital's staff, toward Tom. "I truly can't thank you enough, sir."

Hallett took the executive's hand and gave it as firm a shake as he dared, relieved and admittedly impressed by its strength, noting that the man must be at least well into his fifties. "You're welcome, sir," he said, then quickly added, "I'm glad you're okay, sir."

"As am I," the big man said with a smile, releasing his grip on Tom's hand after giving it an extra, little squeeze. "I apologize for interrupting your day, Mr. Hallett, but my employer and I are firm believers in, for lack of a better term, fate, and upon reviewing your records, I believe that our paths crossing this morning may have been more than a simple coincidence. That's something I'd like to explore if you'd be willing to indulge me for a bit."

Once again, Hallett was immediately stunned anew, not just by the almost-casual but somehow still deeply-respectful manner of the big man's speech, but by the fact that he was clearly, and quite humbly,

13

asking his permission to continue their conversation. Such courtesies were of course completely unnecessary as members of the executive class were effectively allowed and well within their rights to order just about anything from any citizen at just about any time. This being a widely-known and accepted perk of their status, which served as a reward for the extensive burdens of responsibility they bore as the world's ultimate decision makers: revered, held accountable, and potentially punished for every action they took in a way no ordinary citizen ever would be. Thus, Tom had no doubt that a class three executive regularly made several decisions that profoundly affected thousands if not millions of people on a daily basis, and was therefore truly shocked that such a man would actively seek his permission for anything. "Of course, sir," he finally managed after a long pause. "Whatever you'd prefer."

"Excellent," the big man said, then put up a hand, seeming to note something being viewed in his own augmented vision. "Again, my apologies, Mr. Hallett. Another moment if you would," he said, then shifted his attention to the room's door as it opened and an impeccably-dressed woman entered it, two, platinum stars emanating from her lapel pin as she approached the big man's bed, shaking her head but smiling as she spoke.

"You certainly do find interesting ways to avoid promotion, Jacob," she said with a little laugh.

"I assure you, Muriel, this particular incident was completely unintentional," the big man replied, putting his hands up in a faux gesture of surrender.

"Nonetheless," she acknowledged, "this level of carelessness can't be overlooked."

"I understand, old friend," Jacob said, then added. "Do your worst. I deserve it."

The female executive nodded, Tom doing his utmost to not stare agape at her after her abrupt, dramatic entrance, then looked directly at the big man's lapel pin. Immediately, an almost-full, blue circle formed around the three stars it projected, revealing precisely how close he was to advancing to class two status. The circle then turned red, quickly reducing in a sweeping, radial motion to a point just above a third, losing more than half of its capacity as the big man's face contorted in a literal expression of the intense pain being experienced in his mind as he was rapidly and severely demoted.

A single tear escaped the executive's right eye and he quickly brought up a hand to wipe it away as the circle around his rank stabilized, then vanished, his three stars pulsing to reaffirm that his overall status hadn't changed despite his significant punishment.

Her face softening, Muriel leaned over, putting a hand on the big man's right shoulder as she gently spoke. "Please, be more careful, old friend. I'd hate to lose you."

Jacob nodded. "I will. I promise and I'll see you soon, but now, if you'll excuse me, I have work to do." He said this in a way that was decidedly respectful but also surprisingly insistent, as if he were ordering as much as asking it of her.

"Of course," Muriel said with a smirk, shooting a quick look toward Tom. "He's interested in this one, is he?"

Jacob nodded and Muriel put up a hand, clearly not needing or wanting him to respond further. "By the way, I'm taking this opportunity to have a new outfit sent over for you, Mr. Westbrook. I trust that you'll find it acceptable."

"I'm sure I will, Mrs. Westbrook," Jacob said with a smile.

With that, Muriel bent down and planted a gentle kiss on the big man's forehead, then simply said. "Happy birthday, Jacob," before rising back up to her full height and departing.

The big man blushed, immediately bringing his hand up and wiping away the tiny trace of Muriel's lipstick from above his brow before returning his attention to Tom. "Now. Where were we, Mr. Hallett?"

His mind completely overwhelmed by the events of the day, Tom reflexively asked a question he normally wouldn't have dared to utter aloud. "Your wife's a class two?"

"Ex-wife," Westbrook corrected, then quickly added. "Not that that had anything to do with it, I assure you. She's always been a higher rank than me… in a lot of ways."

For a moment, the executive appeared to be lost in thought, which gave Tom's mind the opportunity to fully recognize just how potentially offensive his question had been. "I apologize, sir. It wasn't my place to ask that."

The big man sniffed. "Think nothing of it, Mr. Hallett. It's an unusual circumstance to be sure, particularly in this day and age." Jacob paused as if considering something, then extended his hand toward Tom. "Let's get to know each other a little better before we proceed, shall we?"

Hallett immediately recognized what the big man was proposing, the exchange of personal information via implants being a fairly-common practice between citizens. Of course, Westbrook already had full access to Tom's records by virtue of his executive status, so his offer to make such information about himself available to the archivist was yet another shockingly-generous overture on his part that Hallett immediately felt compelled to accept simply as a matter of good form.

The younger man reached out, firmly gripping the executive's hand and their eyes locked for a moment. In that instant, a wealth of information was transferred to Tom regarding the man before him. In addition to his precise height, weight, and age, Hallett was now fully aware of various means by which Westbrook could be contacted, including the addresses of several homes he owned and the ability to request direct communication with him via their respective implants. He even had access to a real-time if highly-censored version of the big man's calendar, which was essentially packed with a constantly-shuffling collection of events and meetings that were being continuously displaced by the time they were currently spending together.

Indeed, Jacob Westbrook had shared nearly every aspect of his personal and professional life with Tom within reason and the younger man couldn't help feeling a bit closer and more connected to him as a result. "Thank you, sir," he said simply. "That was very generous of you."

Westbrook squeezed Hallett's hand again before letting it go, lifting his palm into a somewhat-dismissive gesture. "It's the least I can do for saving my life, friend." Jacob paused but before Tom could respond to his latest act of kindness, the big man continued. "Now that we've gotten to know each other, I'd like to discuss what happened this morning, if you don't mind."

Hallett nodded, almost delirious from Jacob's obviously-intentional use of the word "friend." "What do you want to talk about, sir?"

"Please, Tom, call me Jacob," the executive said, "at the very least, whenever we speak privately. I insist."

"Okay... Jacob," Hallett said somewhat reluctantly.

"Good man," Westbrook affirmed, "and to your point, I'm particularly interested in this moment."

There was a swish of motion in Tom's augmented vision as Jacob pushed an image captured from one of the cameras onboard the pod they'd both been riding in earlier that morning into Hallett's field of view via the open connection between their implants. In it, Tom could clearly be seen tapping the transparent, soundproof divider separating them just before the big man had begun choking on the nut that had nearly killed him.

"You knew what was going to happen to me, didn't you, Tom?" The big man said this matter of factly, without even a hint of accusation or judgement in his voice.

Still, Hallett immediately blushed, instantly feeling ashamed for not having done more to try to prevent what had occurred despite his next statement. "Not completely," he admitted. "I mean, I wasn't certain of it, not like knowing the sun's gonna come up tomorrow certain, anyway."

At this, Jacob grinned and he raised an eyebrow. "That's an interesting choice of words, Tom, but tell me, on a scale of one to ten, how sure were you and when? I mean, obviously, you were sure enough to tap the divider but when did it first occur to you and how sure were you then?"

Tom thought about it, then shrugged. "About thirty seconds earlier. Pretty much as soon as I saw the nuts in your hand. I knew about the bump in the road and I guess my brain just sort of automatically did the math when I saw how you were eating them, knowing how pods travel that route…" Hallett trailed off, realizing the Jacob was studying him intensely as he spoke, then forced himself to continue. "A seven I guess," he said timidly, then quickly added. "I might have been more sure and put it together quicker but I was… distracted."

"I can't imagine why," Jacob said with another smile, then adopted a more serious expression. "Do you have any idea why I was in old town this morning, Tom?"

Hallett shook his head.

"Any guesses you wouldn't mind sharing? I promise you it's not vital. I'm just curious," Jacob assured him.

"You probably had to talk to someone who doesn't have an implant, someone you couldn't just contact without visiting them in person." Tom said this with a level of confidence a bit more intense and certain than he'd intended but nonetheless felt an immediate surge of pride when Westbrook responded affirmatively.

"That's absolutely correct, Tom. Good man!" Jacob repeated, delivering the phrase in the most positive and complimentary manner the younger man could have imagined. "In truth, Mr. Hallett, I came to old town in search of a legendary storyteller, who politely declined the offer I made to him, but I suspect I may have found one even better in you."

Tom's eyes widened and he immediately shook his head. "I'm no storyteller, Mr.... Jacob. I'm just an archivist!"

"Is that so?" Westbrook said with another grin, then pointed at the little bulge in the breast pocket of Hallett's shirt. "Then, if you don't mind me asking, exactly what's that doing in your pocket, friend?"

For a moment, Tom froze, unsure how to interpret Jacob's statement and deeply ashamed at the realization that the executive had clearly spotted the souvenir he'd taken. Slowly, the younger man reached into his pocket and removed the macadamia nut, holding it between the thumb and first two fingers of his hand. "I'm sorry, Jacob," he said somberly. "I shouldn't have taken it."

The big man immediately put up his hand, waving off Hallett's apology. "Nonsense!" Westbrook said reassuringly. "That just proves you're the right man for the job, if there was any doubt."

Tom responded with a suitably-perplexed look. "Job?"

"Actually," Jacob clarified, "it's more of a mission than a job but I suspect it's one you'll be eager to participate in should it be fully revealed to you."

Completely overwhelmed, Hallett was shocked into absolute, still silence. Was he truly being actively recruited by a class three executive who now willingly and casually called him friend to embark on some sort of "mission?" It was all too much and his stunned face plainly and reflexively showed it.

Seeing this, Jacob smiled again, then laced the fingers of his hands together, resting them on his chest just above his belly. "It's okay, Tom. I know it's a lot to take in but I give you my word, I'll walk you through it all, every step of the way, and if you decide it's not for you, I won't press the issue or bring it up again. Okay, friend?"

"I... I don't know what to say," Hallett admitted.

"I'm sure you have a lot of questions and I'll likely have answers to most of them for you in due time, but for now, the most important question is one I have to ask you. Do you trust me, Tom?"

"I do, Jacob," the archivist said without hesitation.

"Excellent," the executive affirmed. "That's a perfect way to begin." He then flicked his index finger from the side of his head toward Hallett and an address appeared in the younger man's augmented vision. "Meet me there first thing tomorrow and I promise, you won't be disappointed. Deal?"

Tom nodded, then looked down at the nut in his fingers for a moment before extending his arm and offering it to Westbrook, who presented his own hand, palm up, to receive it.

As soon as it made contact with his skin, the big man immediately flicked the nut up toward his fingers with his thumb and grasped it in a similar manner to the method Hallett had used a few moments prior, lifting it to within a few inches of his right eye. "So, we meet again," he said in an even-lower, more-dramatic variant of his potent voice and Tom couldn't help chuckling a bit. Jacob then moved to place the nut on a small stand next to his bed before returning his full attention to Hallett. "Thank you, Tom. That was very generous of *you*," he said sincerely. "Will I see you tomorrow then?"

The archivist nodded with a smile. "Yes, sir. Bright and early."

"Good man," Westbrook said simply, giving him a polite nod and wave as the younger man departed. A few moments later, the executive mentally responded to his employer's voice in his head, looking up at the camera in a corner of the room that constantly watched him. "Yes, sir. Thank you, sir."

"Take the rest of the day off to fully recover, Mr. Westbrook. I will personally see to the items on your calendar to get you back on schedule," the voice proclaimed.

"That's very kind of you, sir," Jacob thought with intense appreciation as the familiar, blue circle reformed around the three stars of his executive rank and filled slightly, sending a brief but euphoric rush of pleasure into his mind before locking into its new, nearly half-full position and disappearing.

"Happy birthday, Jacob," the voice concluded, then severed the connection after making him aware that the room's camera had been temporarily disabled, granting him absolute privacy for an indicated period of time.

At this, Jacob let out a little, involuntary moan of ecstasy, thoroughly stretching his extremities before sinking into the bed's padding and surrendering to a prolonged, blissful sleep, knowing it would likely be the last he'd experience for quite a while, if ever again.

CHAPTER 3

MISSION CONTROL

For the rest of the day, Tom Hallett operated in a sort of haze, returning to work and completing his assigned tasks using a kind of autopilot, born from years of practice and repetition. Occasionally, he absently reached up to the spot on his shirt where the macadamia nut had been, almost regretting his decision to part with it even as he reassured himself that what he'd experienced had actually occurred.

Despite those brief pangs, Tom ultimately felt good about returning the nut to Jacob, realizing that possessing it likely provided a sort of cathartic relief for the older man, which he concluded was a far better and more important thing than it simply serving as a prop to legitimize his own experience, or any tales he might tell of it.

Ironically, Hallett hadn't felt compelled to share any aspect of the story with any of his coworkers, feeling that it was somehow better kept as a mostly-private matter between himself and his new "friend." He supposed that was really the crux of it. To him, Jacob Westbrook was no longer simply a class three executive, almost objectified and placed on a societally-crafted pedestal to be revered, reviled, or ridiculed as needed. He was a fellow man that he "knew," that he'd spent time with and spoken to in a genuine manner, and who he was rapidly realizing he liked and cared for quite a bit as a person. Those acknowledgements it seemed to Tom were the important takeaways from his experience, far more important than any attention or clout he might receive from other citizens by revealing what had happened to them.

Thus, Hallett completed his work day and boarded a pod for home, making a conscious decision to keep his eyes open as the vehicle passed through old town, and paying particular attention to the grand, antique home Jacob had exited when their paths had first crossed as he traveled by it. "In truth," he concluded, "it's really not such a bad place."

The next morning, after a surprisingly long and restful sleep given his perpetual excitement regarding precisely what his new friend had in mind for him, Tom practically sprung out of bed and hurriedly prepared himself to make his way to the address Jacob had provided. As he did so, he confirmed via his implant that he had indeed been "excused from work indefinitely without penalty by executive order," which gave him a giddy, little rush each time he verified the words of the notification in his augmented vision.

Soon after that, Hallett arrived at his destination, staring up at the large, black, monolithic building from the sidewalk where his pod had deposited him in total awe. The structure was completely vacant of any sort of sign, marking, or designation, which ironically clearly identified it as the corporate headquarters of the world's most powerful entity.

Tom took a moment to gather and steady himself, then proceeded, bolstered by the remnants of the confidence still present in him from the previous day's events.

Inside the building's lobby, the archivist was surprised to be greeted by an actual person as opposed to a drone or a simple message pushed into his implant by the structure's security system. The young, suited man, an obvious executive in training indicated by his lack of lapel pin or projected rank, spoke up enthusiastically. "Good morning, Mr. Hallett! If you'll follow me, I'll take you to Mr. Westbrook!"

Tom nodded and the younger man immediately turned, setting a controlled, measured pace through the building and occasionally glancing back to ensure that Hallett was continuing to follow him and not falling behind. They quickly reached an elevator, which automatically opened, and the younger man gracefully gestured for Tom to precede him into it.

"Thanks," the archivist said instinctively as he entered the chamber's sleek, spacious confines, making his way toward its rear before turning to face the other man, who had stepped in just enough to let the doors close behind him as the lift began to make its way skyward.

"You're quite welcome, sir," the executive in training replied, grinning slightly and clearly pleased to be participating in whatever was transpiring.

Realizing this, Tom asked, "Can you tell me anything about what's happening here?"

The younger man immediately put up his hands and shook his head slightly. "Apologies, sir, but even if I could, that certainly wouldn't be my place."

Hallett nodded, understanding the rigid structures of formality that existed in any significant corporation, which were no doubt present in their most refined and potent forms within the building he was ascending.

Still, to Tom's mild surprise, the younger man continued. "I will say, sir, that any project involving Mr. Westbrook is sure to be both exciting and worthy." He then lowered his voice and leaned in toward Hallett slightly. "In truth, sir, I'm thrilled to be involved in any way at all."

At this, Tom considered whether the extent of the man's knowledge and participation in whatever Jacob had in mind for him had simply been a directive to escort him through the building. That certainly seemed possible, which made the executive in training's enthusiasm that much more striking, and served to pique his own interest regarding what was about to be revealed to him.

The archivist nodded and the younger man resumed his normal posture just as the elevator reached the building's 33rd floor and its doors opened with a quiet but still-effective chime. At this, the executive in training backed away and ushered Hallett into a large, otherwise-vacant lobby surrounded by doors where Jacob Westbrook stood at its center, almost at attention, in the finest suit and pair of shoes Tom had ever seen, the three stars of his executive rank almost seeming to blaze as they were projected into the space just beyond his left breast in the archivist's augmented vision.

The younger man finished his gesture, then caught sight of the executive and did an involuntary double take, clearly not having expected to encounter him in person and obviously struggling to maintain his composure, as he stepped back to make way for Tom, who quickly passed him, eager to reunite with his new friend.

"Well done, Mr. Collins," Jacob said with a quick nod. "That will be all, thank you."

For a moment, the younger man was absolutely stunned but to his credit, he recovered quickly, turning to face Westbrook and nodding himself as he slowly backed into the elevator. "Thank you, sir, and thank you for the opportunity," he managed just as the elevator doors began to close, barely spotting the little "thumbs up" gesture Jacob gave him with his actual hand before the corresponding, virtual reward manifested in his vision and mind via his implant when the elevator began its descent.

Westbrook then turned his full attention to Hallett, smiling broadly and extending his hand. "Good morning, Tom. Lovely to see you again, my friend." Jacob almost sang the last bit in a melodic fashion that was unfamiliar to the archivist but a quick search via his implant revealed it to be a reference to a generations-old song by a band called "The Moody Blues."

As he shook Jacob's hand, Tom was briefly tempted to respond with the next line from the lyric, which had been automatically presented to him as a result of his search but refrained, feeling as though it would be disingenuous to do so and a misuse of the technology, not having been familiar with the song, or even its existence, prior to that moment. Thus, he settled for a more-traditional greeting. "Good morning to you, Jacob. You look... fantastic!"

Jacob's smile broadened and he blushed slightly, lowering his head a bit and shrugging his shoulders in an almost-adorable gesture of humility. "Muriel always did know exactly how to dress me," he admitted. "I'll be sure to tell her you approve when I see her. She'll be absolutely tickled."

The archivist laughed a little nervously, still not feeling completely comfortable with the idea of becoming the subject of a class two executive's focus for any reason or length of time, despite his current company. "Is she here?" Tom asked almost timidly.

"Goodness, no," Jacob said with a laugh of his own. "At least, I sincerely hope not. That would be quite a lapse in security!"

Hallett looked at Westbrook in an obviously-befuddled manner and the older man immediately elaborated, clearly not wanting to add to his confusion. "She works for the Pryce Foundation, Tom. Completely different organization."

"Oh," Hallett said. "I thought she must be your boss. You know..." Tom trailed off, making a little circular motion with his index finger to crudely but accurately simulate the diminishing of Westbrook's rank indicator he'd seen the previous day during his demotion."

"Ah," Jacob recognized. "I can see why you thought as much but that was simply a courtesy on my employer's part. Demotions can be executed by appropriately-ranked executives from competing corporations under certain circumstances, mostly to ease or enhance the punishment. It's not done often, especially these days, but I'm grateful that Muriel still cares enough for me to see to it when I occasionally and inevitably do something stupid or foolish." Jacob laughed again. "Trust me. A demotion's way worse when you know the person executing it hates your guts, or is just plain disappointed in you."

Based on what he'd learned of him so far, Hallett found it difficult to believe that anyone could truly hate or be disappointed in Jacob Westbrook but he also supposed that there were many aspects of the corporate world, particularly at the level of it that the Westbrooks inhabited, that would likely always remain mysterious and perplexing to him. As such, he simply nodded.

Apparently content with that response, Jacob shifted his expression and voice to a more serious, formal state before speaking again. "Listen, Tom. As much as I'd love to spend a bit more time easing you into all of this, the fact is that things are coming to a head here and I'm sure you're eager to know exactly what this is all about, so I'm going to cut to the chase if you don't mind."

Again, Hallett nodded, but a bit more enthusiastically to confirm Jacob's analysis.

"Good man," Westbrook said, then flicked his index finger from the side of his head toward Tom's as he had the previous day, sending a long and complicated-looking document into the younger man's mind and field of vision via their implants. "A standard nondisclosure agreement, I assure you," Jacob said as the archivist studied it. "Basically, if you reveal any of what you experience here to anyone without permission, we can destroy your life," the big man said with a little grin.

For a moment, Hallett's eyes widened, realizing that his friend was both joking and being completely serious. "I see," the younger man said, continuing to study the document even as he instinctively requested a legal analysis of it via his implant.

Seeming to recognize this, Jacob spoke again in a more reassuring tone. "Trust me, friend. It's just a formality. I give you my word, I'll never steer you wrong."

Tom hesitated for a moment, thinking back to Jacob asking if he trusted him the previous day and the response he'd given. He then quickly scrolled down to the bottom of the document and applied his digital signature to it.

The big man smiled and nodded, stepping back and waving Tom forward toward a large set of doors behind him before turning to face them.

As Hallett approached, the results of the legal analysis appeared, confirming the document to be precisely what his friend had indicated and nothing more. A moment later, the doors parted and Tom was immediately overwhelmed by the dizzying array of equipment, people, and activity present in the cavernous room beyond them.

The archivist entered the chamber, his eyes immediately drawn to several, immense screens hanging from its ceiling that showed images of the solar system, Earth, and a region of space that at first appeared to be empty, until Hallett registered a small, glowing mass at the center of the display.

The doors closed behind them and Tom looked over at Westbrook, his mouth hanging somewhat agape. "What is all this, Jacob?"

"It's the end of the world as we know it," the big man said flatly, looking back at Hallett with a somber, almost-defeated expression before making an obvious effort to perk himself up, "but we're damn sure gonna fight it. You can take that to the bank!"

CHAPTER 4

NEMESIS

"The truth is," Jacob continued, noting Tom's worried expression, "we don't know exactly what it is. It's some sort of anomaly, there and not there, like a rip in space, or time, or the whole damn universe from what the scientists tell me. Point is, it's dangerous, spitting out all sorts of radiation and other toxic crap, and we're headed straight for it."

Westbrook gestured toward the screen showing the representation of the solar system and it sprang to life, animating to show the planets circling the sun and moving toward the anomaly's indicated position until the image froze with the mysterious mass and Earth nearly at a point of intersection. "That's when it'll be close enough to kill everything on the planet," Jacob said matter of factly and Hallett's blood ran cold. "When is that?" The archivist asked this, barely able to speak.

"About a year and a half from now," Westbrook confirmed.

Stunned anew, Tom swayed on his feet and Jacob reached out to steady him. "Easy, friend. You're almost through the worst of it. Just hang in there, okay?"

Hallett looked at the big man, utterly baffled and astounded by his ability to achieve and maintain any semblance of calm in the face of such knowledge. He then put his own hand on Jacob's shoulder, hoping to draw on his obvious strength and forcing his mind to shift to a more analytical, less emotional mode of operation to prevent a total breakdown. "It looks bigger," he finally managed, pointing to the screen himself.

"Indeed," Westbrook said. "It's growing at an exponential rate," he confirmed, then gave the archivist's shoulder a little squeeze. "That's why we have to stop it, Tom, no matter what, or we'll just be the first thing it destroys."

Hallett looked at the executive incredulously. "Me? What could I possibly do about... that?" He asked this emphatically, deeply concerned that his new friend had grossly overestimated him to the possible detriment of humanity itself.

"Easy, Tom," Jacob said reassuringly. "This won't be on you at all. In fact, all the important decisions have already been made."

At this, Hallett relaxed a bit, letting his hand fall off the big man's shoulder, and immediately began to feel more steady on his feet. "Then, why am I here, Jacob? Why show this to me?"

The executive nodded and smiled. "Because, Tom, we need someone to tell the story of all of this. To a person, everyone here is completely focused on the task at hand as they must be but inevitably, and sooner rather than later, the world will know about all of this and someone will eventually need to share the details of it with them, assuming that we're successful."

For more times than he could easily recall, Tom Hallett had been shocked into motionless silence over the past twenty-four hours but none of that could have prepared him for the absolutely gobsmacked state Jacob Westbrook's words had triggered. In his wildest, most-ambitious fantasies, Tom had never even imagined himself being in such a position. On some level, a tiny fraction of his mind was able to acknowledge that there was some sense in the idea of a professional archivist being tasked with observing and recording the details of such a monumental event but the notion that he of all people could possibly be the most skilled or worthy to do such a thing was simply ludicrous beyond comprehension to him. Still, as he stared dumbfounded at Jacob Westbrook, Hallett could just as clearly see another truth in his eyes. The man before him undoubtedly believed in him and his ability to do what was being asked of him, conveying it to the younger man in the confident, compelling way that only a high-ranking executive could.

"You really think I could do that, Jacob?" The archivist asked the question despite his observation, both needing to hear the response aloud and admittedly unable to think of anything else to say in that moment.

"Of all the things that are happening right now, Tom, that's the one I'm most certain about, for what it's worth," Westbrook confirmed.

With that, Hallett set his jaw and made his decision. "Where do I start, friend?"

CHAPTER 5

WALKING WITH THE REVELATOR

Walking through the mission control area of what he had been casually informed was simply called "The Nemesis Project," Tom could clearly see that Jacob Westbrook was completely in his element. As he confidently strode from station to station, the heels of his polished, leather dress shoes potently and distinctively clacking against the finished, concrete floor, even amid the constant drone and bustle of their surroundings, the big man calmly and thoroughly explained the purpose of everyone and everything in the room.

In truth, the broad strokes of the project and its intent were deceptively simple. In orbit above the Earth, a spacecraft, the first and perhaps last of its kind, was being hastily constructed with the intent of delivering a team of specialists to the anomaly to analyze and eliminate it as a threat to Earth and the surrounding universe at any cost before the point of fatal intersection.

Of course, there were literally millions of subtle and nuanced details and potential points of failure to consider in such an endeavor and Tom soon found his mind swimming in a sea of technical jargon and heady, scientific concepts that were admittedly well beyond his ability to fully, or in some cases even partially, comprehend.

Still, Hallett did his utmost to keep up with Jacob, understanding more than ever that every moment the executive was spending with him was a moment he inherently couldn't spend elsewhere. Of course, Tom also understood that Westbrook was almost certainly multitasking to a degree, using his implant to receive and respond to any number of notifications and queries while they spoke in much the same way ordinary citizens regularly did in interactions amongst themselves. Even so, the archivist remained impressed with just how much direct and personal attention Westbrook was clearly providing to him. Seeing his interactions with others in the room and their consistently-respectful, almost awestruck responses to his approach, Tom realized just how overwhelmed and incapable of functioning in Jacob's presence he would have been had he first encountered him in that setting.

As the tour neared its end, Westbrook introduced Tom to Robert Briggs, the man who had largely designed and would act as the chief engineer of the ship being sent to intercept the anomaly. The apparently diminutive but full-faced man popped his head up from behind a counter where he'd been rummaging at the sound of Jacob's approach and greeted him with a broad smile, his short, spiky hair only conveying a sense of order due to its meager length. "Good afternoon, Mr. Westbrook!"

For a moment, Hallett was perplexed by the greeting, not realizing how much time had passed since he'd first entered the facility early that morning. He was about to indicate as much aloud when the older man, perhaps in his mid to late thirties, stood up completely, a large rifle in his hands.

Immediately, Tom was filled with an intense panic, having only ever seen images or virtual representations of such firearms and being well aware of their potential, destructive power. He recoiled instinctively, taking a couple, abrupt steps backward but quickly composed himself, seeing that Jacob was completely unfazed by the development.

"Good afternoon, Bob," Westbrook said with a nod and a smile of his own. "Is that a new iteration?"

The younger man nodded enthusiastically. "Yes, sir! Care for a demo?"

"By all means," Jacob replied. "I'm sure our new archivist, Mr. Hallett, will be particularly interested."

"Archivist!" Bob exclaimed excitedly, removing a hand from the gun and extending it to Hallett, giving the younger man's appendage a thorough and enthusiastic shake. "About time you got someone in here to witness all this!" He chuckled, focusing his attention completely on Tom. "Two things, Mr. Hallett: You call me Bob. There's only one guy I let call me Mr. Briggs. No offense, Mr. Westbrook!"

"None taken," Jacob said simply.

"Tom," Hallett offered, completing the handshake.

"Well, that oughta be easy enough," Briggs noted. "You stick with me, Tom, and I'll fill that head of yours up real quick." The engineer let out a laugh, leaning back a bit as he returned his full grip to the gun.

Jacob rolled his eyes a little but gave Tom a look indicating that he was actually quite fond of Briggs and his mannerisms. "If you please, Bob, we're in a bit of a hurry," the executive said politely.

Briggs immediately put up a hand and nodded, continuing to grin as he made his way over to a stack of metal panels leaning up against the wall of his work area, picking up one with a large, scorched hole in it and moving to place it in a clamp that automatically opened and closed to leave it suspended vertically in the air above his workbench while humorously feigning annoyance. "Yes, Mr. Westbrook. Right away, Mr. Westbrook!"

The executive chuckled a little himself, taking a step back and folding his arms over his chest in a traditional expression of patient anticipation.

Seeing this, the engineer ceased his banter and adopted a more serious demeanor, focusing his attention on his task. He moved to a position about ten or twelve feet from the plate, then spun a large dial on the side of the gun until a tiny light on it turned yellow and it emitted a series of sounds indicating some sort of mechanical process taking place within it. This was accompanied by a low-frequency hum that quickly swept up to a higher pitch, holding it for a moment before the weapon fell silent again.

Briggs then shouldered the rifle, aiming it straight at the hole in the plate before squeezing its trigger for a moment.

Instantly, there was a potent sound of an electrical discharge and a spherical, glowing, yellow mass ejected from the gun's wide barrel, maintaining its form until just before it reached the hole when it rapidly expanded, filling the gap and removing any sign that it had ever been damaged in seconds.

Shocked in his now-customary fashion, Tom tentatively approached the plate, maneuvering to carefully examine it from both sides and failing to find any sign that a hole had ever existed in it. "Unbelievable," he said simply.

"Very nice, Bob," Jacob agreed.

The engineer shrugged, "I adjusted the dispersion rate and recalibrated the payload sensor so there are fewer wasted nannies. It's not perfect but it's close. It'll all be in my report, assuming that you still read those."

"I assure you that I do, Bob," Westbrook said sincerely. "Every word, and well done, as usual."

"Thanks, boss," Briggs said, then seemed to recall something, hurrying back behind the counter and stowing the rifle before retrieving a much smaller object and extending it up and out toward Jacob in one hand, letting it fall and dangle several inches from a long, elastic loop as he came to a stop a few feet in front of the much larger man.

Even before the item's movement slowed to a gentle, pendulum-like sway, Tom recognized it as the macadamia nut that Jacob had choked on the previous day, which had been coated with a spherical, glossy, transparent substance and embedded into the center of a wide, thin, silver medallion with an intricate pattern of fine grooves etched into it. The overall effect made it vaguely resemble a ringed planet akin to Saturn and the executive whistled in an obviously-impressed manner as his eyes focused on it and he moved to secure it in his own grasp. "That's wonderful, Bob! Even better than I imagined. Thank you!"

"Anything for you, boss, you know that," the engineer affirmed, releasing his grip on the necklace's loop and letting it pass into Jacob's hand. "I'm glad you're okay, by the way."

Jacob nodded, then draped the loop over his head and began tucking it under the collar of his dress shirt with one hand even as he continued to examine the details of the pendant while holding it with the other. "Thanks to Mr. Hallett's efforts," he said simply and Tom blushed a bit when the engineer nodded approvingly in response.

Westbrook used the hand that had been tucking in the elastic to pull the front of his collar and his tie away from his throat just enough to slide the medallion beneath his clothing, allowing it to come to rest against his skin at the center of his chest between his breasts. He then looked down, returning his collar and tie to their normal, ideally-positioned states and confirming that the object's presence beneath his suit was completely undetectable. "Perfect," he said simply.

Briggs nodded but nonetheless offered, "Just let me know if anything needs adjusting. I wasn't entirely sure how it'd feel under... all that," he admitted, gesturing to Westbrook's elaborate outfit before patting his own basic but practical attire.

Jacob shook his head, "It's completely comfortable, Bob. I assure you. Thanks again!"

The engineer put up a hand in an almost folksy, "'tweren't nothin'" sort of expression then returned to his work as he concluded, "Nice to meet you, Tom. I'm right here if you gents need me!"

With that, Westbrook gave Tom a little nudge and they proceeded along their way, Hallett simply waving to Bob in response, not wanting to distract him further.

When the pair had moved off to a more-secluded corner of the room, Jacob stopped, turned to face Tom, and simply asked, "Any questions?"

In point of fact, Tom Hallett had no shortage of questions despite the mountain of information that had been bestowed on him over the past several hours but his mind was still struggling to process and properly order all of them, so he settled for the most-recent one he could recall. "Nannies?"

Westbrook laughed a little. "Ah, yes," the big man acknowledged. "That's Bob's little nickname for the nanites, arguably the Pryce Foundation's most important contribution to this effort."

Tom nodded but persisted, feeling certain that Jacob had considerably more to reveal regarding the technology, which had arguably been the most-impressive thing he'd seen in a day full of impressive things. "What are they, exactly?"

"It's a bit complicated," Westbrook admitted. "They've been sitting on that tech for decades, slowly and carefully refining it. The core of it's a real Pandora's Box, the kind of thing that could cause a lot of problems in the wrong hands, which is why they've been reluctant to roll it out but given the situation..."

Again, Tom nodded but maintained eye contact with Jacob, giving him what he reasoned was a solid, "come on, friend, spill the beans already" look.

Westbrook chuckled again. "You really are perfect for this job, Tom," he acknowledged before obliging him further. "In a nutshell, they're autonomous, microscopic machines that operate in a variety of capacities based on how they're initialized. They all start out the same, in their inert, grey state, where they can be used for fuel or filtration. Once activated, the green and yellow ones can repair organic or inorganic structures respectively as you saw. The blue ones can attach to objects or each other and generate fields of various types that let them temporarily shield or block an area for example. And the red ones..." Jacob paused for a moment as if carefully considering his words. "Those little bastards can kill or destroy just about anything you fire them into, only stopping when they reach an assigned limit, or encounter a different substance than their initial target, or they're deactivated. Actually, there are several more, and very necessary, failsafes for them but you get the idea."

When Jacob Westbrook had been on the verge of his collapse just outside their pod the day before, Tom had seen a pure, unfiltered expression of terror on his face as he'd silently pleaded for his assistance. Since then, the big man had consistently manifested a seemingly ever-increasing air of confident composure but in that moment, Tom saw a brief flash of that same sort of fear return to his face. Clearly, he reasoned, the red nanites in particular were nothing to be trifled with. "I understand," Hallett affirmed and the executive nodded, indicating that he believed the archivist truly did.

After a brief pause, Jacob continued, seeming to note something in his augmented vision. "If you don't mind, Tom, I believe we've covered enough for your first day."

Admittedly relieved, Hallett nodded decisively, immediately recognizing just how mentally exhausted he'd become and conscious of the fact that he would likely benefit from at least some time alone to process everything he'd experienced.

"Great," Westbrook confirmed, then lifted a finger, pointing to a small drone that rapidly descended from the ceiling and took up a position a bit behind Tom's right shoulder. "I want you to go home and pack up anything you think you might need for the foreseeable future. You can bring it with you tomorrow or just stack it up and we'll see to its delivery for you. From then on, I want you here with the rest of the team."

When Hallett didn't immediately respond, the executive quickly added, "Don't worry. The accommodations here are quite spectacular. You definitely won't be roughing it."

Tom shrugged, a somewhat befuddled expression on his face. "It's not that, Jacob. I'm sure they're wonderful. I guess I just realized that I work for you now."

"Is that a bad thing?" Westbrook asked sincerely.

"Not at all," Hallett said reassuringly. "Everything's just happening really fast," he admitted.

"That's why I'm giving you an escort," the big man said, pointing to the drone again. "I know you'd never intentionally jeopardize what's happening here but we all make mistakes. This little guy will keep an eye on you and make sure we know if anything gets out so we can handle it."

Tom's eyes widened slightly.

"Don't fret, friend," Westbrook assured him. "We've had a lot of practice keeping this secret over the years. Nobody will get hurt, even if you somehow manage to flat out break the NDA. We just need to make sure nothing slips through the cracks. Once you're settled in here, this little fella won't be necessary. That said, it'll definitely make things easier if you can keep a lid on all of this yourself, okay?"

"Sure thing, boss," Hallett said with a little grin.

"Good man," Jacob acknowledged and they cordially parted ways, the executive clearly diving headlong into a new series of tasks even as he turned and purposefully began to walk away, leaving Tom to more-slowly and vaguely make his way out of the facility at his own pace, his new escort in tow.

As he entered a pod bound for his home for what he realized might well prove to be the last time, Tom Hallett noted that absolutely none of the data his implant had collected throughout the course of the day since signing the NDA had been transferred to the cloud, having been automatically restricted to his own mind by the parameters of the agreement. Indeed, the archivist rapidly concluded that if he should choose to share any of that information with anyone else, he would have to do so verbally, or through other, antiquated means. Of course, Tom had no intention of doing any such thing, fully comprehending the magnitude of the secret he'd been made privy to and at least some of the potentially-terrifying and destructive consequences revealing it to anyone might invoke.

Thus, Hallett once again returned home in silent isolation, confirming that his previous employment contract had been terminated without prejudice and a new one established by executive order. For the rest of the day and well into the evening, Tom simply spent his time packing and thinking, crafting occasional, carefully-worded messages to family and friends informing them that he would likely be largely unavailable for the foreseeable future due to work-related obligations.

CHAPTER 6

DAY 2

The next morning, Tom awoke with a start from a vague nightmare that quickly and thankfully escaped his mind. He imagined that most if not all of the members of the Nemesis Project suffered similar nocturnal visions, the intense, inherent stress of the knowledge they possessed, much less that associated with any needs or obligations related to it, no doubt being a persistent, nearly-constant burden to them. Still, he felt surprisingly rested and eager to return to mission control, hurriedly making himself presentable while his escort continued to watch over him as it had throughout the night.

The end result of his packing had amounted to two large boxes, mostly containing clothing, and a duffle bag with an outfit for the following day amid a few personal items he felt he might eventually miss if they were left behind for too long. For a moment, Hallett considered leaving the bag with the boxes and simply having the whole lot sent for but decided that it would be easy enough for it to accompany him in a pod. Thus, he indicated as much to the transit system when he scheduled his trip to ensure that a vehicle with sufficient space would be dispatched to him.

When he arrived at the facility's lobby, Tom was once-again greeted by Mr. Collins, who seemed to pay no attention at all to his little, drone escort, which continued to discreetly follow from a bit above and behind Hallett's right shoulder. The younger man now sported his own lapel pin, projecting a simple, white "XXXVI," the lowest-possible executive rank.

"Congratulations, Mr. Collins!" Tom said sincerely.

"Thank you, sir!" The younger man replied, speaking just as enthusiastically as he had the previous day. "I'm deeply honored to have been promoted, and by Mr. Westbrook no less!"

"That's wonderful," Hallett acknowledged, realizing just what a

35

long road the man before him would have to carefully walk to even approach the level his new friend occupied, and that he may well never even get the chance to do so, but still genuinely happy for him. "That happened right after you left us?" Tom asked, pointing to the pin.

Collins nodded, then shook his head slightly. "I got the notification in the elevator but Mr. Westbrook wasn't available for the ceremony until almost midnight." He then paused, perhaps realizing that some or all of what he was saying might find its way into Jacob's head. "Not that I'm complaining, sir! I would have waited all night or longer. It was a true honor! I knew I was close but I had no idea I was that close!"

"Well, congratulations again," Hallett said, then added, seeing that the new executive had become lost in his own thoughts. "Do you by chance have a message for me, Mr. Collins?"

Immediately, the younger man snapped to attention. "I sincerely apologize, sir! I believe I'm still a bit delirious but that's no excuse. Please, if you'll follow me, I'll show you to your quarters, then to Mr. Westbrook."

Tom nodded, "It's quite alright, Mr. Collins. No harm at all, I assure you." Hallett said this in a completely-soothing and convincing way, feeling as though he understood exactly how the younger man felt despite a part of him recognizing that might not be strictly true.

"Thank you, sir!" Collins replied, immediately accelerating into motion as if attempting to make up for lost time despite Tom's insistance.

A few minutes later, Collins ushered the archivist into the most spacious and luxurious living quarters he'd ever seen, which were far in excess of his own, humble abode. Hallett whistled, quickly making his way around the various rooms and confirming that the area only contained a single, large bed. "This is all for me?" Tom nonetheless asked upon returning to the living room, his duffle bag still slung over his shoulder.

"Absolutely, sir," Collins confirmed. "We have a few minutes if you'd like to settle in or we can make our way to Mr. Westbrook at a more leisurely pace if you'd prefer." He then added, noting Hallett's expression of indecision, "There are some other facilities you may find interesting along the way."

"Sure," Tom agreed, letting his bag slide off his shoulder and to the floor in a controlled manner. "By all means, Mr. Collins, give me the grand tour!"

The younger man nodded and they soon made their way through a series of nearby rooms containing a dining area, a fitness center, and a variety of other amenities that would no doubt make anyone's stay on the building's 23rd floor, which appeared to be entirely dedicated to such purposes, as comfortable and convenient as could reasonably be expected.

In a decidedly-efficient manner, Collins completed the tour and saw Hallett to the elevator, delivering him to the 33rd floor as he had the previous day, and far less shocked to find Jacob Westbrook patiently waiting in the lobby for them.

Once more, Collins stepped aside, just outside of the elevator, making way for the archivist's exit, this time looking directly at Jacob as Tom passed him to await any further instructions.

"Thank you, Mr. Collins. That will be all for now," Westbrook said with a nod.

For just a moment, the younger executive seemed to hesitate, perhaps missing the additional bit of overt praise he hadn't received for completing his most-recent task but did not linger, quickly moving to the elevator as he replied, "Thank you again, sir, for everything!"

The doors closed in front of Collins and he couldn't help feeling a little dejected at his superior's lack of further acknowledgement. He was just about to conclude that he was likely being unreasonable in his expectations when a tiny blue sliver formed around the outside of his rank indicator and grew ever so slightly before disappearing, sending a brief but euphoric rush into his mind as a result of his first executive promotion. "Thank you, sir!" Collins thought excitedly. "Thank you very much!"

Back in the 33rd floor's lobby, Tom noted that Jacob looked a bit tired despite continuing to project his normal, convincingly-powerful and commanding presence. "Good morning, Jacob!" He said enthusiastically, hoping to bolster his friend with some of his own energy, which seemed to work as Westbrook appeared to perk up slightly.

"Good morning, Tom. Lovely to see you again," Jacob offered in a slightly-truncated but still somewhat-musical repetition of the previous day's greeting.

Having listened to the song, and in fact the entire album, he'd become convinced Westbrook was referencing while drifting off to sleep the previous night, Hallett confidently elaborated. "Shall we walk to the next bend?"

"Indeed," Jacob said with a broad grin, lifting a finger to dismiss Tom's escort, which darted off into a vent near the ceiling that automatically opened to make way for it. He then added, "I'm pleased to inform you that no incidents were logged by your little companion. Well done, friend, not that I had any doubts."

Tom shrugged. "It was surprisingly easy, once I realized what was at stake."

Westbrook nodded, "Still, give yourself some credit. That was a lot to take in and hold onto and you certainly wouldn't have been the first to crack, or let something slip, if you had. Hell, if you were an executive, that performance would have merited a nice, little promotion."

Hallett blushed slightly, taking Jacob's statement for the compliment he was certain it was intended to be. "So, what's on the agenda today, Mr. Westbrook?"

Jacob set his jaw for a moment, then nodded, seeming to internally confirm his decision before making Tom aware of it. "I believe you're ready for the next level," he said gregariously, putting an arm around the archivist's shoulders as he gently led him toward one of the lobby's side doors. "Let's head over to the lab, Mr. Hallett!"

CHAPTER 7

THE LAB

In a stark contrast to mission control, the 33rd floor's lab environment was strikingly sedate and placid, comparatively almost devoid of apparent sound and activity. As such, Jacob made an obvious effort to tread more lightly as they maneuvered through it to the work area of Dr. Monique Maxwell, the project's lead scientist.

Tom was immediately struck by her obvious youth and her classically-attractive appearance, doubting that she could possibly be much older than himself. Indeed, Hallett rapidly concluded that she was even more captivating than the "pretty lady" from his old pod route and thus made a particular effort not to stare or unduly admire her when they were introduced.

"When it comes to the anomaly and what we know of it," Jacob concluded, "you won't find anyone on Earth more knowledgeable."

Monique smiled slightly but also shrugged. "For what that's worth," she admitted. "Unfortunately, we've largely reached the limits of what we can test and observe from here. I fear there isn't much more we can do without more direct access to the phenomenon."

Westbrook nodded, the information clearly not being new to him. "Fortunately, we've managed to largely stay on schedule. You won't have much longer to wait, Dr. Maxwell, I assure you."

"I know everyone is doing their absolute best, Jacob," she said reassuringly. "It's just frustrating to think we might reach a point where even a moment is wasted."

As if on cue, a soft chime sounded, indicating that the results of a test the scientist had been conducting were available. "Speaking of which. If you gentlemen will excuse me..." she said politely.

"Of course," Jacob replied, gesturing for Tom to follow him out of the area. "Please include Mr. Hallett as a recipient of your reports to me moving forward."

"Absolutely, sir," Maxwell acknowledged, already beginning to study the data her workstation had automatically presented to her as soon as her eyes had focused on its screen.

Again, Tom found himself impressed and somewhat awed by the scientist's focus and calm. Indeed, it truly seemed that everyone involved in "The Nemesis Project" was just as determined and steadfast as its administrator. Hallett supposed that made sense. After all, Westbrook's company clearly had no shortage of resources or will to use them but it was still heartening to see such a large group of people operating with such an obvious intent toward the good of humanity and everything around it. "How did you find all these people, Jacob?" Tom asked as they made their way to a different area of the lab through a series of decontamination zones. "I mean, I can't imagine a traditional job posting would suffice." Hallett chuckled slightly, considering how such a description might read. "WANTED: Someone to save the world. Must be extremely intelligent, capable, and not prone to panic."

"Actually," Westbrook replied, "you're the only person I've actively recruited. My boss selected everyone else."

Tom's mouth fell open for a moment before he managed to fight the reflex and close it. "Seriously? You didn't have any say in it?"

Jacob nodded, "In truth, I'm extremely grateful to have been spared that burden," he admitted. "Moreover, my employer was the first to become aware of the threat the anomaly posed, well in advance of anyone else on the planet. He was therefore uniquely qualified to make such decisions and in fact specifically cultivated and nurtured the careers of nearly all of the team members for years with this particular project in mind."

Hallett whistled, "So, we're in good hands then?"

Westbrook immediately nodded. "There are none better, I assure you."

Tom paused briefly, letting that sink in, then somewhat-tentatively asked, "Can I meet him?"

"Absolutely," Jacob affirmed, "but not right now. As I'm sure you can imagine, he's extremely busy but I promise you, your paths will certainly cross before too much longer and he's absolutely eager to make your acquaintance." The executive paused, then continued, seeming to carefully choose his words. "He's quite pleased that you've decided to join us."

Tom nodded, satisfied for the moment but more curious than ever about Jacob's employer, who had almost miraculously remained mysterious and largely sequestered from the world despite decades of wielding more power than anyone else in it and being known, if only by name, to all of its occupants.

As those thoughts played out in Hallett's mind, the duo reached their destination where they found two technicians, Rashid and Steve, who were in the process of testing a prototype for an unorthodox "artificial gravity" system that was to be used to allow the ship's passengers to move about it more normally than would otherwise be possible in open space. Rashid, the senior of the two techs, briefly explained to Tom that the effect was produced by a series of tiny conduits integrated into the ship's deck plating and other key surfaces to distribute blue nanites that could be activated and deactivated at will, adhering and releasing objects to and from those surfaces based on perceived exertions of force to vaguely approximate Earth-standard gravity.

"Basically," the tech concluded, "the little guys can see your foot coming down toward the deck and will attach you to it until you take a step, then time and execute their release in a manner that gives you the feel of gravity. Think magnetic boots but way more sophisticated and they can attach to anything, automatically adjusting their grip and release based on the sort of object they come in contact with and the forces at play.

"Care to give it a try, Mr. Hallett?" Steve asked, clearly eager to show off the technology as he ascended into a mockup of one of the ship's corridors with its nearest wall missing.

Tom looked at Jacob, who quickly nodded. "Go right ahead. It's actually kinda fun."

Reassured, the archivist didn't hesitate, stepping up into the faux corridor with Steve, who nodded to Rashid as Tom got into position. "Since we're still on Earth," Steve explained, "we'll just give you a taste of what the little guys can do. Go ahead and walk down the hall."

Hallett complied, his first couple steps feeling perfectly normal, but as Rashid made adjustments on his console, Tom quickly found it increasingly difficult to pull his feet from the floor with each stride. To him, it felt a bit like walking through deepening water or snow and by the time he reached the end of the hall, he could feel the muscles in his feet and legs starting to burn. "That's crazy!" he exclaimed, looking down at the deck plates for any sign of the nanites that had been pulling on his feet but nothing was visible.

Steve nodded, then pointed to a flashlight amid a cluster of tools attached to a portion of the wall next to Tom that had a similarly-textured surface to the floor beneath him. "Go ahead and pull that torch off," the tech encouraged.

Again, Tom did as he'd been told and removed the flashlight from the wall, feeling even more strongly that it must have been attached to it magnetically.

"Now, throw it back at the wall," Steve instructed.

Tom looked at the tech incredulously.

"Go ahead," Steve insisted. "Chuck it as hard as you can."

After seeing the nods of the other men around him, Tom brought his arm back and threw the flashlight with what he reasoned was enough force to possibly damage it and was astounded when a slew of barely-visible, glowing, blue threads ejected from the wall, captured the flashlight, and compressed to bring it to a gentle stop before disappearing completely as they affixed it to the vertical surface.

"Unbelievable!" the archivist acknowledged, struggling to decide which application of the nanites that he'd seen was more impressive.

Again, Rashid worked his console and the tools all fell from their places on the wall at Tom's feet. When the archivist instinctively moved to back away, the nanites under his shoes pushed off against them, causing him to jump up and away twice as far as he'd intended.

The other men in the room chuckled a bit as Hallett struggled to regain his balance, his wide eyes indicating precisely how astounded and caught off guard he'd been.

"Sorry, Mr. Hallett," Rashid said a bit sheepishly, completely deactivating the system and turning his display toward Tom to assure him of its state. "I couldn't resist!"

After taking a moment to recover, the archivist laughed a bit himself. "It's okay. No harm, no foul!"

Jacob stepped forward and offered a hand to Tom as he descended back to the lab's floor. "You actually got off easy, friend. You should've seen what these two jokers did to me the other day," he said with a little snort.

At this, Steve blushed particularly conspicuously. "Sorry again, Mr. Westbrook. You're not still mad about that, are you?"

"You're still here, aren't you?" Jacob said with a bit of a stern look, then smiled. "As Mr. Hallett so effectively put it, Mr. Cox, no harm, no foul."

"Thank you, sir," Steve quickly replied, clearly relieved.

Westbrook nodded. "Okay, gentlemen, back to it. I trust this little demonstration won't affect your overall productivity for the day, will it?"

"No, sir," both techs immediately replied, almost in unison.

"Good men," Westbrook affirmed, then directed Tom toward the area's exit, following closely behind him.

As the pair traveled through another area, Tom observed several, large, pill-shaped objects that vaguely resembled what he imagined coffins might look like if such things were still commonly used enough to warrant continued evolutions of their design beyond what had been traditional in the past. He believe he recognized them from one of Jacob's previous descriptions but nonetheless felt compelled to confirm his assessment. "Are those the gravity couches?"

"Indeed, they are," Westbrook affirmed somewhat excitedly. "You really have been paying attention, haven't you?"

"To every word, I assure you," Tom said with a smile, pleased that his assessment had proven correct even as he noted a single, significantly-larger container amid the others that he reasoned might represent a prototype or previous iteration of the technology.

"Good man," Westbrook acknowledged in his customary fashion as they made their way out of the lab and back into the floor's lobby. Again, Tom noted just how tired his friend looked despite his efforts to conceal it while he obviously acknowledged yet another notification that had been pushed into his field of view by his implant. "Apologies, Tom, but I believe that's all we'll be able to cover today. Please, take some time to rest and enjoy the accommodations, then meet me here tomorrow morning and we'll continue with the medical facilities and personnel. I assume you won't have any difficulty navigating the building on your own after Mr. Collins' thorough efforts."

"Of course," Hallett said confidently, "but shouldn't you get some rest yourself?"

Westbrook shook his head. "I appreciate your concern, friend, but I'll have an opportunity to catch my breath soon enough. Until then, anything less than everything I have is unacceptable." He then put a hand on Tom's shoulder. "I'll be alright, Tom. I promise."

Convinced if not totally reassured, Tom made his way to the elevator, briefly looking back at Westbrook as the big man purposefully made his way back toward mission control, his footfalls returning to their typical, penetrating volume as he approached its opening doors.

CHAPTER 8

NOCTURNAL ADMISSIONS

That night, Tom found himself standing in one of the ship's completed corridors, staring down its length toward a bright light that somehow wasn't as blinding as his mind reasoned it should be.

From out of that light, Jacob Westbrook emerged and began walking toward him, a grin of satisfaction on his face. Immediately, the archivist noted a distinct lack of sound, indicating that he'd somehow been deafened. As the executive approached, his pace slowed and Tom became aware that the older man was increasingly struggling to advance with each step, his face contorting into an expression of pain and frustration, until the big man's elaborate shoes became effectively fused to the deck plate beneath him, halting his progress.

Obviously perturbed, Jacob bent down and untied the Oxfords, stepping out of them and collapsing to one knee when his socked, right foot became similarly affixed to the ground. Again, his expression morphed into one of wide-eyed fear and panic, his hands raising in a defensive gesture as he silently mouthed the words, "No! Please! Don't!"

Hallett looked down at his own hands, one of the nanite guns loosely held in them. In a detached, almost-mindless manner, his right hand reached for the rifle's dial and turned it until a little, red light appeared on the weapon.

In front of him, Westbrook began screaming and violently shaking his head as he repeatedly tried and failed to free himself from the ground, his hands trembling in the air in front of him. Jacob then looked up pleadingly, tears welling in his terrified eyes as his mouth hung open in an expression of total shock and dismay.

Numbly, Tom adjusted his grip on the rifle and vaguely pointed it at Jacob before pulling the trigger.

Instantly, a mass of red nanites ejected from the gun's barrel and struck the executive in the chest, rapidly spreading and devouring him, clothing and all, until only a faint cloud of ash and spent nanites remained, immediately falling and disappearing into the floor's intricate network of tiny holes.

Tom screamed, staring at Jacob's empty shoes, the only evidence that his friend had ever existed, then woke with a start, sitting bolt upright in his bed on the 23rd floor and drenched in sweat.

Immediately, the archivist sent out a ping, attempting to connect to Jacob's implant and establish communication with him.

A moment later, a text message appeared in his augmented vision. "In a meeting. Is it urgent?"

Immediately relieved, Tom replied in a similar fashion. "No. It can wait. Sorry to bother you."

"No bother at all. Good night, friend," came the almost-instant reply.

Having been thoroughly awakened by his nightmare, Tom made his way into his living unit's shower, then got dressed and ventured to the floor's dining area, hoping to find a midnight snack to soothe his mind and take it off the disturbing images he'd experienced that were uncharacteristically lingering there. "I would never do that," Hallett assured himself. "Ever, no matter what!"

In his fully-rational, conscious state, Tom was sure that was absolutely true and he could certainly see how some wires could have gotten crossed in his subconscious after the events of the past few days in a way that could have led to the vision but it still troubled him deeply. As much as it pained him to admit it, Tom Hallett had never had a true, close friend. To be sure, he'd had playmates as a child, peers as a teenager, and colleagues as an adult, but he'd never managed to cultivate and maintain a relationship with anyone as intense or meaningful as the one he was forming with Jacob Westbrook. Consequently, he was truly disturbed by the idea that he might possibly do anything, consciously or unconsciously, to harm or jeopardize it in any way. As he reached the dining area, it therefore occurred to Tom that his dream may well have been a direct response to that very fear, which seemed increasingly likely the more he considered it.

Inside the large room, Hallett was somewhat surprised to find a man, smartly dressed in traditional chef's attire, patiently waiting behind a prep station. Immediately, the older man made eye contact with him, nodded, and gestured for him to approach. "Good evening, sir. What can I do for you?"

Tom realized that the man likely hadn't been standing there all night, the building's automated systems almost certainly having informed him of the archivist's approach, perhaps only moments before it had occurred, but the effect was still impressive as had clearly been intended. "I'm just a little hungry," Hallett admitted. "Maybe a little something sweet, and something to help me get back to sleep."

The chef nodded. "Right away, sir. If you'd care to have a seat, I'll be with you in a moment." The man gestured, indicating that practically any location in the area, which was almost entirely empty, was available to him.

"Thanks!" Tom replied with a nod of his own, then made his way to a large, unoccupied table near a pair of women who were engaged in a quiet conversation but not so close as to potentially overhear them.

The archivist settled into his comfortable chair, putting a hand on his head and giving it a thorough rub until the vivid images of Jacob's horrified face and his shoes sitting untied and vacant on the deck plate finally dissolved into obscurity in his mind. Tom reasoned that they wouldn't truly be gone and forgotten for a while but he was nonetheless relieved that they'd retreated as quickly and readily as they had.

A moment later, the chef arrived, placing a small glass containing what appeared to be slightly-steaming, warm milk on the table in front of him and displaying a large tray filled with several, small pastries of various types.

Hallett briefly examined the options, then selected a little coffee cake, removing it from the tray as the chef provided him with a fork and a napkin from it with his free hand. "Very good, sir," the older man affirmed. "Is there anything else I can bring you?"

"No," Tom said simply. "This is perfect. Thank you!"

The chef nodded and quickly departed, leaving Hallett alone with his thoughts.

The archivist picked up the fork and took a bite of the cake, quickly concluding that it was the best of its kind he'd ever had. He supposed that shouldn't have been a surprise but still remained equally impressed when he took a sip of the milk and found that it had been infused with one or more additional ingredients that made it far more appealing and effective than he'd expected it to be at first glance. "These people really do know exactly what they're doing on every level," he thought, his archivist brain inherently understanding better than most just how much individually-subtle details were apt to create a cumulative effect in a variety of circumstances.

As he casually completed his snack, one of the women at the nearby table stood and made her way over to him, her shoulder-length, red hair appearing somewhat out of place as if she'd had her own sleep similarly interrupted but not felt compelled to address it. "At the risk of stealing Jacob's thunder, I wanted to introduce myself," she began with a smile, extending a hand to Hallett, which he quickly shook. "Sophia Fields, mission commander," she added.

"Pleased to meet you, commander," Tom said sincerely, having been informed of the crew members he'd yet to encounter by Jacob and certain that they'd been similarly informed regarding him by that point. Still, he completed the formal introduction in what he hoped was an appropriate and sufficiently-respectful manner as if Westbrook were standing next to him. "Tom Hallett, archivist."

Fields nodded. "Trouble sleeping, Mr. Hallett?" she asked, then quickly added with a smile, "If so, welcome to the club!"

The archivist nodded, her admission undoubtedly making him feel a bit more comfortable about doing so. "It's been a lot to take in and process," he acknowledged.

"No doubt," Sophia affirmed, then laughed a little. "Still, if you're feeling up to it and you'd like to get a jump on things in a less-formal setting, Dr. Clay and I will be here a little while longer." Fields gestured to the other woman, a decidedly reserved and contemplative expression on her face amid her short, dark hair, even as she lifted a hand to wave at Tom in response.

Hallett pondered for a moment, returning the gesture before replying. "Actually, I believe I'm scheduled to tour the medical facilities with Mr. Westbrook in the morning." He paused, then added with a laugh of his own, "I'd hate to steal his thunder."

Sophia smiled. "Fair enough, Mr. Hallett. By all means, get some sleep while you can. We'll all be wishing for it soon enough, I'm sure."

"No doubt," the archivist confirmed, standing and looking about for a likely place to deposit the remnants of his meal, only to see the chef rapidly advancing toward him, clearly indicating his intent to address the mess himself. "Good night, commander," Tom concluded.

"Good night, Mr. Hallett," Sophia replied, returning to her place with Clay and resuming their conversation.

CHAPTER 9

ON THE THIRD DAY

To his relief, the rest of Tom's sleep was decidedly uneventful and he once again found himself feeling surprisingly rested and energized when he awoke the following morning. As such, he quickly prepared himself and made his way to the 33rd floor a few minutes before the block of time on Jacob Westbrook's calendar that indicated their scheduled meeting.

Admittedly, Tom had been a bit curious to know if he'd find Jacob standing in the lobby as he'd apparently been the previous two days when he'd arrived or if the big man simply had his schedule so finely tuned that he would appear moments before their meeting was to commence. Thus, he wasn't entirely surprised when the elevator doors opened to reveal the vacant lobby and stepped out into it confident that his friend would soon arrive. Even up to the last few seconds before the stroke of nine o'clock, Hallett remained convinced that Westbrook would enter the room, perhaps in a rush, and assume the position he'd typically occupied almost at attention before commencing their business but as soon as the hour arrived with no sign of the executive, Tom immediately felt a twinge in his gut and became intensely concerned.

For several minutes, the archivist actively fought the urge to ping Jacob's implant, not wanting to give in to the rapidly-increasing panic and dread he was feeling as the images from his nightmare slowly but steadily crept back into his conscious mind. "He's okay," Tom insisted to himself. "He's just running late, or stuck in another meeting. He'll be here. He promised me he'd be alright." At that thought, Tom chided himself, realizing just how childish a thought it was. If something had happened to his friend, the correct response certainly wouldn't be to think of it as a broken promise. Hallett therefore made a concerted effort to calm his mind and focus, resolving to give Jacob at least a few more minutes before attempting to contact him and vowing to only act in a reasonable and considerate manner regardless of the outcome.

A few more minutes passed and Tom managed to stay true to his intent, achieving and maintaining a legitimate calm as he rationally considered the steps he might take to locate and assist his friend if necessary, utterly refusing to allow himself to even consider the possibility that the executive was anything other than alive and well.

Finally, about a minute before the time he'd internally concluded represented a reasonable delay, one of the lobby's previously-unused side doors opened and Jacob Westbrook strode out of it, an apologetic look on his face. "I'm very sorry to keep you waiting, Tom, but it couldn't be avoided."

"It's okay," Hallett replied, raising a hand in the dismissive gesture he'd seen Jacob use dozens of times by that point and beyond relieved to see him. "I know how busy you are."

Westbrook shook his head but nonetheless acknowledged. "That's very kind of you. Good morning, by the way."

"Lovely to see you again," the archivist offered and the big man smiled, all at once looking as vibrant and energized as ever.

"You too," Jacob said simply, then quickly added, "Listen, Tom, a lot has happened in the past few hours that I have to tell you as it's going to affect our day but before we proceed, what did you want to talk about?"

Hallett paused, considering what if any of his dream he wanted to reveal to his friend. On one level, it suddenly felt completely irrelevant and unimportant, particularly given Jacob's apparent news and the fact that the executive was standing right in front of him, looking as well and fit as ever. Still, the archivist had no desire to lie, or keep anything from him, so he looked away slightly and sheepishly said, "It's nothing. I was just worried about you."

At this, Westbrook put a hand on Hallet's shoulder and gave it a little squeeze until he gained his full attention. "Never be ashamed for caring about people, Tom. It's one of your best attributes."

"Thanks, Jacob," Hallett said, resisting the urge to inform the executive that it was, indeed, specifically him that he cared about in a way that he'd never experienced before.

With that, the big man nodded, removed his hand, and continued with the business of the day. "We've known for a while now that it was only a matter of time before someone outside of the project detected the anomaly. That happened last night."

"Oh," Tom managed, all of his mind's energy and effort immediately shifting away from his own concerns and toward the obvious implications of that development. "That's not good."

Jacob nodded. "Obviously, we're doing our best to handle the situation but the proverbial cat is definitely on its way out of the bag at this point, so we need to accelerate our efforts a bit, which means we'll have to skip the tour of medical, among other things, as they're already in the process of packing."

"Does that mean what I think it means?" Hallett asked, a lump forming in his throat.

"Indeed," Westbrook affirmed. "We're moving up the timeline, which means the team has to deploy immediately, as in today."

Tom already had a vague understanding of what that meant from Jacob's previous revelations. He knew for example that all the key personnel and equipment that were destined for the ship would be leaving the building and making their way to a launch site, where a small armada of reusable rockets was on standby to deliver them to orbit.

"I guess we're headed to the launch site then," Hallett offered somewhat confidently but the big man immediately shook his head.

"I would have loved to be there for the launch, Tom, but I have to stay here to coordinate things in light of what's happened," Westbrook corrected in a resolute but almost-sorrowful manner.

"You want me to go there alone?" Hallett asked incredulously.

Jacob laughed a little. "Well, it'll be rather difficult for you to get to the ship otherwise and you most certainly won't be alone."

Westbrook's words ricocheted inside the archivist's mind like pinballs for a moment as he realized that his friend was being completely serious. "You want me to go... up there?"

The big man shrugged, "That was always the plan, Tom, but I admit, it would have been preferable if I'd had a bit more time to ease you into the idea."

"I... I... thought I'd be here, archiving everything from mission control... with you," Hallett admitted.

"That's certainly possible, Jacob acknowledged, "but you'll never get a better view or sense of what's actually happening than you will on that ship, if you're up to it that is."

"I don't know if I can do that, Jacob," Tom said, again lowering his voice and looking away slightly.

"For what it's worth," the executive offered, "I know you can." He then added after a short pause, "And the truth is, I'd feel a lot better about all of this with you up there, keeping an eye on things for me. Still, it's your call, friend, and I'll back you either way."

Again, Hallett looked directly into Jacob's eyes, seeing the same expression of assured certainty he'd always conveyed when informing him of anything and Tom knew without question that the big man truly did believe in him and would remain his friend no matter what he chose to do.

Indeed, a significant part of him wanted to immediately agree, simply to help and please the man, who'd so clearly put such a tremendous amount of faith in him, but the archivist was equally full of fear, not only of what might happen to him on an unproven ship attempting arguably the most dangerous task in the history of humanity, but of what might happen to Jacob in his absence.

For a time, Tom Hallett simply closed his eyes, allowing his archivist mind to rapidly run through all the possible scenarios that might unfold in either case. In the end, he realized that the choice had to be his and made for his own reasons given the consequences it would no doubt produce. He therefore took in a deep breath, opened his eyes, and informed Westbrook of his decision. "Okay, Jacob. I'll go."

"Excellent!" The big man exclaimed, clearly relieved as he rushed forward, wrapping his arms around the archivist and lifting him off the ground in a massive bear hug. "I truly can't thank you enough, Tom!"

"Think nothing of it, buddy," Hallett said, artificially distorting his voice even more than it already had been in Jacob's grasp for comedic effect as he felt the subtle lump of the big man's macadamia nut pendant pressing against his own chest through their clothes.

CHAPTER 10

DEPARTURE

The next few hours were a whirlwind of activity as Tom did his best to keep up with Jacob while the executive buzzed around the 33rd floor, ensuring that everyone there had everything they needed. This culminated in a brief meeting with the entire team gathered in mission control, which proceeded in an almost shockingly calm and business-like manner as Westbrook quickly ran down an enormous checklist of items, confirming himself or receiving confirmation from one of the others present that they had all been properly addressed.

Finally, the big man stood, lacing the digits of his hands together but keeping the two index fingers extended as every pair of eyes in the room focused on him. "In truth, I could search for the rest of my life and never find the words to adequately express the respect and admiration I have for each and every one of you and the work you've done here. Whatever the outcome, know that you have undoubtedly done more to ensure our survival and future than any in history and on behalf of those who may never know the efforts and sacrifices you've made, I sincerely thank you for all of them." He paused for a moment, looking around the room, then nodded. "Now, let's go save the world!"

Immediately, the room exploded in a cacophonous eruption of enthusiastic applause and cheering as several team members approached Westbrook, patted him on the back, and shook his hand. For his part, the executive remained largely stoic and reserved in his customary fashion but nonetheless smiled broadly as the circle around his three-star rank indicator revealed itself and quickly filled to almost its full capacity, stopping just short of advancing him to class two status. At this, Tom couldn't help but laugh at the seemingly-arbitrary metrics used for executive promotions and demotions. In his mind, Jacob's efforts as the Nemesis Project's manager were clearly deserving of far more praise than his boss had seen fit to bestow on him, especially given the half a rank he'd lost for accidentally choking on a nut, but again, Tom was forced to conclude that he simply lacked the context to fully assess or appreciate the act. Indeed, it occurred to him, even amid his befuddled annoyance, that the system was likely designed to make promotions difficult to earn and demotions easy to incur to keep executives on their toes and discourage deviant behavior or complacency. He further decided to file the thought away and enjoy the moment, hoping to potentially discuss it with Jacob's employer given the opportunity, being well aware as most were that he and his family had been largely responsible for the system's creation, refinement, and acceptance throughout the world.

After allowing the congratulations and revelry to continue for another minute or so, Westbrook put up his hands and the room immediately fell silent again. This time, instead of speaking, Jacob simply extended his hands a bit further, simultaneously dismissing everyone in the room and effectively ordering them back to work without a word.

"That's real power, wielded perfectly," Tom thought, as impressed as ever by his friend but also finding himself almost desperately curious to witness his superior in action. With that in mind, he approached Jacob and respectfully asked, "Where do you want me, boss?"

The big man nodded, then gestured toward Hallett, waving him forward as he backed away toward the engineering area before turning and pointing at Robert Briggs. "You stick with Bob like glue, Tom, and he'll take good care of you. I promise."

"Will do. Thanks, Jacob," the archivist acknowledged, admittedly a little disappointed by the realization that he'd likely be leaving the facility without getting the opportunity to meet with Westbrook's employer. Clearly, like his scheduled tour of the medical facilities, that item had been struck from the agenda in light of recent events.

Still, Hallett dutifully made his way toward Briggs, only stopping next to Westbrook when the executive put a hand on his shoulder and gave it a squeeze in his typical manner to get his attention before speaking. "Thank you again... for everything, friend. I'll see you soon."

All at once, Tom was almost overwhelmed by the notion that he very well might never see Jacob Westbrook again, in person or otherwise. For an instant, he couldn't breathe, much less speak, but he willed himself to do both, desperate to not let the opportunity pass. "You can count on it, Mr. Westbrook," he said as confidently as he could, putting his own hand on the big man's shoulder and giving it a squeeze that he hoped at least approximated the intensity of the older man's grip.

"Good man," Jacob said simply. "Good man."

From his nearly-empty work area, Briggs called out to both of them in a half-joking, half-serious manner that put a smile on each of their faces. "If you two are done having a moment, I could use a little help carrying the rest of this crap!"

With that, Tom Hallett was on his way, barely noticing Jacob's retreat to the heart of mission control after the big man picked up one of the remaining items in Bob's area and handed it to him as the engineer began to directly engage the archivist in conversation.

Unexpectedly, Hallett found himself eager to do so and grateful for the apparent effort Briggs was making to ease his transition into his care. Tom had thoroughly appreciated and enjoyed Bob's friendly, "no nonsense" demeanor during their first interaction and quickly discovered that the man was quite a conversationalist, and surprisingly able to speak effectively on a variety of subjects beyond those of a strictly-technical nature. In short, he rapidly concluded that the engineer was just the sort of well-rounded yet obviously skilled and intelligent fellow one would ideally want in such a position. He briefly wondered if the decision to pair them had been Jacob's or his boss's but quickly determined that it didn't matter, knowing that Westbrook had undoubtedly endorsed and been comfortable with the idea regardless of its origin.

Within an hour, Briggs and Hallett were speeding along in one of the company's private, jet black pods toward the launch site.

At about the halfway point, the vehicle stopped briefly to collect the one member of the ship's primary crew Tom had yet to meet, Major Adrian Pryce III, who would act as both its tactical officer and military liaison. Tragically, his father, who'd held the rank of Colonel and been the one originally selected for the position, had been seriously injured in a training accident and forced to resign his commission just a few months prior. Fortunately, the younger Pryce had already been selected and partially trained as a backup, and had been more-or-less able to quickly step into his father's role. Indeed, the ship would still carry at least one backup for each key position, who would remain on standby in a mostly-dormant state within the protected confines of a gravity couch to be called upon if needed, one of Pryce's Air Force colleagues having been assigned to the backup position once he'd been promoted out of it.

Again, Tom found himself a bit bemused by the fact that there was no such contingency in his case, Jacob having assured him that he would be the project's one and only archivist, not because the position was any less important, but because he believed him to be singularly qualified for it. As ever, that thought simultaneously filled Tom with equal measures of pride and fear and Hallett made a conscious effort to keep both emotions in check and focus on his task.

By the time they reached the launch site, formal introductions had been completed and the archivist had begun to get a sense of Pryce, who immediately struck him as a practical, "no nonsense" sort akin to Briggs but decidedly less friendly and warm in his mannerisms. Clearly, the man had the somewhat cold and calculating mind of a tactician, which Tom supposed was ideal for the position he occupied. Still, it made for a slightly-less comfortable conclusion to the journey as Hallett couldn't help feeling like he was being constantly evaluated and assessed by the new arrival.

When they entered the launch facility proper and their pod eased to a stop near the base of the rocket that would soon take them into orbit, Tom cursed himself for missing the single, previous opportunity he'd had to take such a flight in his early twenties. While certainly not commonplace, brief trips to low orbit and even extended visits to stations in high orbit and beyond in reusable vehicles of various types had become common enough that the archivist's apprehension about engaging in one was fairly mild. Still, he couldn't help thinking it would be one less element of the scenario to worry about if he'd experienced such an event even once before.

Seeing his concern, Bob gave Tom a reassuring pat on the shoulder. "Don't sweat it, Mr. Hallett. I've been up dozens of times and it's no big deal." He then leaned in and lowered his voice a bit. "It's actually quite a rush and I don't mind telling you, it gets me a little hard like clockwork."

The archivist laughed. "Thanks for sharing, Bob."

"Any time," the engineer concluded with a grin, then motioned for Hallett to follow him toward the launch tower's elevator.

As they walked, Tom noted that there were a total of eight, massive rockets, each no doubt carrying a portion of the personnel and equipment destined for the ship high above them. He reasoned that this was likely a necessity given the sheer amount of cargo that had to be moved but also couldn't help thinking how tragic and catastrophic it would be if even one of the rockets and its contents were lost in the attempt.

With what he'd come to realize was their typical calm and business-like efficiency, the members of the Nemesis Project completed the loading of the rockets and their other, associated preparations. Within an hour, Hallett, Briggs, and Pryce were all sitting in the crew module, strapped into their seats amid every ounce of cargo the vehicle could safely carry in addition to their weight.

Indeed, by the time Tom had settled into his seat and began to feel at all comfortable in his new environment, there was less than a minute before liftoff. For an instant, the archivist felt a brief surge of panic, realizing that he'd left his duffle bag in his living quarters back on the 23rd floor but just as quickly sighed with relief when he saw it tucked into a nearby rack, imagining that Mr. Collins had been tasked with its retrieval, perhaps earning himself another little promotion for successfully reuniting it with its owner.

Noting the position of his head, Bob tapped the archivist on the shoulder and pointed straight up toward the ceiling above them, which featured a display that showed the sky beyond the rocket's nose. "Keep your head straight, Mr. Hallett, or we'll be taking you right to Dr. Clay for a new neck when we arrive." The engineer chuckled a bit but gave Tom a stern look, indicating that he would do well to heed his advice.

The archivist quickly nodded, then put the back of his head firmly against the headrest as the countdown reached its end.

A moment later, the loudest, most-forceful thing he'd ever experienced smashed Tom Hallett into his seat as the rocket quickly made its way skyward. For a time, the archivist could barely breathe as his eyes watered uncontrollably but as the vehicle's velocity increased and the linear force of its upward movement normalized, Tom was at last able to catch his breath enough to scream, "No big deal, my ass, Bob!"

Next to him, the engineer laughed, triggering a mild coughing fit until he held his breath and fell silent, the broad grin on his face expanded by the force being applied to it as he struggled to give Hallett's leg a couple reassuring pats. "Hang in there, Tom," he choked out. "We're almost home!"

CHAPTER 11

THE APEX

A few seconds later, the rocket's main engine cut out and separated, beginning its rapid yet calculated descent back to Earth as the crew module's significantly-smaller drive ignited to lift the vehicle the rest of the way into orbit.

Instinctively sensing that the most-dramatic and risky aspect of the journey had been completed successfully, Tom slowly began to relax and focused on the display above him, which was divided into a few sections that showed a variety of information including a rendering of the trajectories of all eight rockets and their separated boosters, as well as the ever-darkening and increasingly star-filled sky they were hurtling toward.

"Unbelievable," the archivist said simply, profoundly moved by the experience.

"It is something," Bob admitted, discreetly making a slight adjustment to his crotch as he caught his own breath, "but trust me, you haven't seen, or felt, anything yet."

Hallett looked at the engineer a bit incredulously, finding it difficult to imagine an experience more intense than the one he'd just had.

In response, Briggs reached out and tapped a control on a smaller screen in front of him and the image of open space on the larger screen above them was replaced by a live view of the ship they were rapidly approaching.

In some ways, the craft was decidedly simple and unimpressive in its design, essentially appearing as a long, grey, rectangular box with an obvious, almost crude-looking wedge distinguishing its front from its rear, but as they approached, the subtleties and details of its hull and its enormous size became more apparent. Indeed, as one of the other crew modules accelerated out in front of them and entered the camera's field of view on its way to dock at the ship's far side, Tom could truly appreciate its scale and complexity. Thus, he sat in rapt attention, observing the vast array of channels, conduits and equipment that had been no doubt meticulously positioned along nearly every inch of its surface, with only a few, obviously-intentionally-smooth areas present in stark contrast.

"Beautiful," Tom indicated, completely awestruck.

"That's my girl," Bob said proudly, then quickly added. "Welcome to the Apex, Mr. Hallett!"

Tom had of course heard the ship's name before but hearing it uttered by its creator, and seeing it presented in such a grand fashion, the archivist was forced to conclude that it was as apt a moniker as any he could have conceived, arguably the pinnacle of what humanity was capable of willing into existence. "That it is, Bob," he quietly acknowledged. "That, it is."

Within minutes, the eight crew modules had docked, four along each of the Apex's lateral surfaces, and each crew began to disembark, unloading their respective contents and making their way onto the larger ship.

Tom did his best to contribute to the effort but admittedly unsure of what should be done in what order, he largely deferred to Briggs, who provided occasional, calm and carefully-worded instructions to keep him productive and on task until only his duffle bag remained in the module's cargo area.

"Go ahead and grab that and I'll show you where to stow it until the initial system checks are done," Bob instructed.

Hallett nodded, gently pushing off one of the cabin's walls and floating over to the bag before retrieving it and repeating the process to return to the older man at the airlock connecting the two ships.

"You're getting your space legs quicker than most," the engineer acknowledged. "Lots of people struggle with zero G at first."

"It definitely feels odd," Tom admitted, "but not as odd as I thought it would."

Briggs nodded, "Just a heads up, I tweaked the artificial gravity a bit now that we've got everything unloaded, so be careful with the transition."

"Thanks for the warning," Tom said appreciatively as he extended his legs beyond the portal and let his feet come to rest on the Apex's deck plating. At first, the sensation was decidedly unnatural and awkward, causing his head to swim a bit, but as he acclimated and took a few tentative steps, the system automatically adjusted to his efforts and Tom soon found himself able to walk around in an essentially-normal fashion without much effort at all. "Nicely done, Bob. I could almost forget we're in space."

The engineer shook his head, indicating that he felt the archivist was being too generous in his praise, but nonetheless agreed, "It'll do, and it will get better once we get moving and the system collects more real-world usage data. Lab tests and simulations can only do so much."

Tom nodded in acknowledgement but found himself immediately distracted by the large, open area they were entering, which schematics of the ship he'd seen casually referred to as the "green room." While that was an undoubtedly-accurate description, the archivist couldn't help feeling that it had drastically undersold it. All around him were a wide array of plants that had been grown over months, perhaps years, clinging to an elaborate network of metal trellises, which created symmetrical, organic pathways through the environment. In the room's center, there was a large, circular pool containing billions of inert, grey nanites that slowly churned from some unseen force being applied to them below a slightly-larger domed ceiling that projected an artificial, blue sky, convincingly reminiscent of an idyllic day on Earth.

"Amazing," Hallett managed, realizing that he was indeed running out of words to properly express his recurring astonishment.

Briggs nodded. "It's a shame it won't survive the trip but it definitely helped to keep the poor bastards who had to spend months at a time up here building all this from going stir crazy." He chuckled a bit. "Some of 'em ended up calling it the zen room, so I guess it was worth the effort, and the plants do help ease the load on the environmental system. That makes it a nice, little win-win in my book and we've gotta take all of those where we can get 'em, right?"

"No doubt," the archivist replied, allowing his gaze to linger on the room's impressive blend of nature and technology even as Bob led him out of it toward the ship's aft, engineering section.

CHAPTER 12

VELOCITY

To Hallett's surprise, the inside of the Apex proved much smaller and easier to traverse than its external appearance had indicated. Indeed, it had only taken them a minute to reach engineering via a small chamber that housed the ship's primary O2 exchanger and a collection of wall-mounted environmental suits that could be used in the event of a hull breach.

It was at that time, carefully making his way through the area's dim and comparatively-cramped confines, that Tom noted Pryce's departure. Clearly, the major had opted to make his way to his own station on the ship's bridge, which wasn't particularly surprising, but Hallett once again noted the man's decidedly aloof behavior, finding it a bit unsettling that he was unable to pinpoint the precise moment when he'd vanished despite a sincere effort to recall it.

"Adrian doesn't talk much," the archivist noted as they'd made their way into engineering and down a set of stairs, the large chamber spanning both of the ship's decks.

Briggs nodded. "His dad's a bit more chatty but there's a healthy dose of 'shut the hell up unless you have something important to say' baked into that bloodline for sure." The engineer shrugged, then added, "I guess it comes from being a descendant of a legend. I can't even imagine trying to fill Conrad Pryce's shoes and he was dead and gone decades before I was even born. That's what I'd call leaving a mark on the world, and a hell of a thing to live up to, whether a fella wanted to or not."

"Yeah," Hallett acknowledged, being well aware of the Pryce Foundation's significant contributions to the world at large long before learning of its unique, and particularly vital, additions to the Nemesis Project. At the thought of the nanites, something clicked in Tom's mind and he immediately felt compelled to verify it with the engineer as he looked around the room. "It's funny, Bob. I didn't realize just how much of the ship was dedicated to storing nanites."

The engineer immediately nodded with a grin, tapping a nearby screen a few times to call up a cross-sectioned diagram of the ship that presented a view from its side. "As you can see, over three quarters of the internal volume went to the nanite tanks, and they all-but surround the crew compartments, aside from the airlocks and a few reinforced and shielded conduits. That's so the uninitialized nannies can filter or neutralize as much as possible of whatever vile crap the anomaly spits out at us that makes it through the outer hull while we approach. Without that barrier, we'd be dead long before we even got close, not to mention all the little guys we're going to have to burn as fuel to get there as quickly as possible."

Tom had already felt reasonably confident that he'd known and understood at least some of that prior to Bob's explanation but was nonetheless grateful and relieved for the confirmation. "And that's why we rushed up here so fast once the cat was out of the bag, right? To take advantage of Venus being so close?"

Again, Briggs nodded. "Exactly! With Venus basically at perigee, its closest possible point from the Earth, we can get a nice, little gravitational boost from it on our way to the sun shot and save a bunch of nannies to use as shielding instead of fuel. Basically, another win-win, but one we would have done without for a little more prep time if that had been possible," the engineer admitted.

Tom pondered that, wondering if the decision to accelerate the mission's timeframe had been the correct one, but rapidly concluded that he both lacked sufficient information to make a proper assessment and was extremely thankful such a weighty dilemma hadn't fallen on his shoulders. "Lemonade out of lemons, I suppose," the archivist concluded.

"Indeed," Briggs confirmed, giving him a quick pat on the shoulder. "Come on, Mr. Hallett. You can give me a hand with the system checks while Rashid and Steve are busy helping everyone else."

Back in mission control, Jacob Westbrook stood, scrutinizing both the large displays above him, which were divided into dozens of unique but related images, and the constant stream of information being presented by his implant in his augmented vision. For the most part, things were going almost shockingly well. The crew and all the remaining equipment had been safely delivered to the Apex before any real chaos had started to unfold on the planet's surface and in point of fact, the initial reactions to the news of the anomaly's "discovery" by the majority of the world's powers had been decidedly measured and restrained. That being the case, there had also already been several, troubling incidents, including the drastic, public demotions, and a few outright executions, of various, prominent executives. These had apparently been carried out to appease various populations eager to lay blame for what they perceived as a failure to identify and address the threat sooner.

In particular, Jacob found a news feed from China of a class one executive being drug out onto a stage, rapidly demoted through all thirty-six ranks, and reduced to a quivering, drooling mass before being shot in the head by a uniformed soldier profoundly disturbing. He knew that the man had likely been effectively killed by the time his rank had fallen to six or seven, demotions of more than five ranks at a time being all-but-certainly fatal. Nonetheless, the big man couldn't help imagining the poor soul somehow managing to survive the ordeal, only to be snuffed out after being reduced to an utterly helpless and broken shell, likely for no real fault of his own.

Such possibilities had of course occurred to Westbrook and his employer when considering what to reveal of the anomaly and to whom over the years, constantly weighing the pros and cons of such actions and doing their utmost to ensure the best possible outcome for all concerned. Still, as ever in life, there had been no perfect solution and Jacob found himself deeply moved and dismayed by every negative outcome he saw unfolding before him in spite of his best efforts. "I'm sorry, sir," he said under his breath as the news footage ended, then willed himself to refocus, desperate to not miss an opportunity to potentially aid the developing situations when possible as he became aware of them.

Mercifully, one of the theories the best minds on his team had conceived did appear to be proving true for the most part. "The Nemesis Effect," as they called it, was simply the idea that faced with such a catastrophic, globally-threatening event, the majority of people would ultimately feel compelled to avoid taking actions that would make the situation worse, particularly when given the option to observe the actions of those attempting to resolve the issue. Therefore, mission control, in conjunction with the US government, had begun broadcasting information and updates regarding the Nemesis Project almost immediately after news of the anomaly had reached the masses.

So far, the effect had been largely positive but Westbrook had no illusions, understanding perhaps better than anyone on Earth how much depended on what was yet to occur. With that in mind, he established communication with the Apex to confirm that they were still on schedule.

"Commander Fields," the big man began, "if you have any good news, I'd be quite happy to receive it."

A moment later, the reply came as Sophia's face, framed by the various electronics along the back wall of the bridge of the Apex, filled the most massive screen's largest section. "The board is green up here, Mr. Westbrook. System checks are completing and we should be getting underway shortly."

"Godspeed, commander," the executive said simply.

"That's the plan, Jacob," Sophia replied with a little grin, then added. "Telemetry… engaged."

With that, the Apex began actively transmitting to mission control, a function that had never previously been enabled to help conceal its presence in orbit. Almost instantly, several new banks of information appeared on the enormous display, the image of Fields automatically shrinking to make room for them.

Westbrook sighed with relief, seeing nothing of concern in the new information, even as a few reports of civil unrest in various locations around the world were pushed into his vision. They temporarily covered part of the mission control data, creating a bit of a jumble, but he quickly dismissed them, concluding that there was nothing he could do to address the issues beyond what he was already doing.

Abord the Apex, Tom studied the engineering display Bob had led him to, confirming and calling out values as Briggs worked with related equipment and occasionally queried him. In many ways, the archivist was grateful to have something specific to focus on, knowing that he likely would have been overwhelmed and effectively paralyzed by his potential choices if left to his own devices in such a scenario, particularly given the lack of time he'd had to prepare for it.

Soon, the checks were complete and the men made their way to the bridge along one of the two, long corridors on either side of the ship's lower deck, passing the science lab, a narrow corridor leading to the primary nanite storage tank, the gravity couch chamber, and the ship's medical facility. Each room was impressive in its own right, packed with equipment and panels that displayed a dizzying array of information, but Hallett did his best to stay focused, not wanting to risk a possible collision with another crew member by letting his gaze linger on any area for too long.

When they entered the bridge, Sophia immediately turned to face them. "Are we good to go, Bob?"

"Indeed, we are," Briggs replied confidently, tapping a screen along the bridge's back wall until it reconfigured to display engineering-related data and controls.

Fields nodded, then spoke directly to the entire crew via their implants. "Attention. Hold position and prepare for acceleration."

In Tom's augmented vision, a simple prompt appeared asking, "Are you ready?" The archivist responded in the affirmative and a few seconds later, a slew of blue nanite tendrils erupted from the floor and wrapped themselves around his legs and abdomen, gripping him snugly as the ship's main engines fired and he felt a tremendous surge of force when it accelerated from a dead stop to a steadily-increasing speed that would soon begin to cover kilometers in seconds.

"TVI initiated," Briggs said simply. "We're off to the races!"

"TVI?" Tom quietly asked.

"Trans-Veneutian Injection," the engineer replied matter of factly. "A little nod to the Apollo program."

"Ah," Tom said, immediately shocked when his implant didn't automatically pull up historical information about the first manned missions to the moon, instead displaying a tiny but still somewhat-jarring "No signal" indicator in the upper-left corner of his vision. "Of course," he realized. "We're off the network, literally above and behind all the transceivers, and can only link with each other." He'd objectively known that would happen to the crew but again, not having expected to be a part of it, he hadn't done anything to prepare himself for the potent feeling of isolation he was suddenly experiencing. Moreover, he found himself acutely disturbed by the notion that he'd no longer be able to access any information about Jacob or communicate with him in any way without making use of the ship's systems. "Easy, Tom," the archivist thought. "You can do this. You're not alone."

Outside, the ship rapidly slid out from over the parabolic structure that had been built to conceal it, making the area appear as the sky behind it would when viewed from the ground, and briefly emerged into existence for all the world to see. Quickly, it accelerated up to interplanetary transit velocity and effectively disappeared, carrying its crew many times faster than any human beings had ever travelled before.

CHAPTER 13

A TOUCH OF VENUS

As the Apex's acceleration stabilized, the blue nanites holding the crew in place quickly retreated back into the deck plating and they were all once again able to move about the ship normally. As promised, Tom noted that the artificial gravity effect did indeed feel a bit more consistent and convincingly Earth-like per Bob's prediction.

"So, how long to Venus?" The archivist asked this of the engineer, even as he stole a look at the older man's screen, hoping to make the determination himself.

Briggs responded, keeping his own eyes on the display while it cycled through a variety of information, unable to present every data point he'd requested all at once. "Assuming that we're able to maintain a full burn for as long as we planned, we should arrive in a little less than a day."

At this, the archivist's eyes widened. "Seriously? How's that even possible? I mean, doesn't it take longer than that to get to the moon?"

"Normally, yes," the engineer confirmed. "Hell, back in the day, it took the Apollo modules over a week to go that far but its really just a matter of resources. It's actually not that hard to haul ass in a straight line, especially once you're already in space. We've been shipping nannies up here for years, so we've got more than enough in the tanks at this point. It's really more about maintaining control and being able to maneuver and slow back down when we need to."

"So, we could have gone straight to the anomaly if we had to?" Tom asked, even as he attempted to work through the scenario himself.

"Technically, yes," Bob agreed, "but we would've used up almost all our nannies just getting up to speed and slowing the hell down once we got close. This way, we'll get most of our acceleration from Venus, and the sun shot, and will only really have to burn the poor, little guys up to hit the brakes."

"How fast are we actually going to go?" The archivist wondered aloud.

"By the time we get to Venus, we'll be at well over ten million kilometers an hour. By the end of the sun shot, we'll be at about a hundred million, or ten percent of light speed, give or take."

"I don't know if I can really wrap my head around that," Tom admitted.

"Think of it this way," the engineer offered. "It takes the light from the sun less than nine minutes to reach Earth, so, when we're going full tilt, we could get back here in say an hour and a half, assuming we exited at the right trajectory and could actually stop in time," Briggs concluded with a laugh.

The archivist whistled. "So, we're gonna have to start braking pretty soon after the sun shot, aren't we?"

The engineer nodded. "Pretty much. We'll be flat out for a bit, which should give the folks at home a nice show, but yeah, a longer, slower deceleration burn is definitely preferable, assuming that nothing unexpected pops up in our way."

Again, Hallett's eyes widened for a moment. "That could happen?"

Briggs shrugged in response. "Sure. I mean, we've done our best to keep an eye on everything that might cross our path but in case you haven't noticed, space is a big place and there's a surprising amount of crap flying around in it." He then added, noting the archivist's obvious concern. "Don't worry, Tom. It's highly unlikely."

"Like choking to death on a macadamia nut," Hallett thought but simply nodded, allowing the engineer to completely focus on his work.

To Tom's mild astonishment, the journey to Venus proved decidedly uneventful, giving him an opportunity to more thoroughly explore the ship and interact with the rest of the crew as they went about their business. He even had a chance to speak privately if briefly with Jacob after transferring his duffle bag from the locker he'd crammed it into in engineering to its proper place in the shared crew quarters at the front of deck two, adjacent to the green room.

Unsurprisingly, the executive looked more haggard than ever, a drone clearly being used to capture his image at close range as he stood in mission control. Still, the big man immediately perked up a bit when he saw Tom appear in a corner of his augmented vision, asking almost playfully, "Enjoying the ride, Mr. Hallett?"

"Absolutely," the archivist replied, grinning a bit despite being slightly vexed by the somewhat-delayed transmissions, which already took several seconds to span the ever-increasing distance between them. "This really is a spectacular thing, Jacob. No one could ever deny it."

Westbrook nodded. "Here's hoping it does the job."

"I know it will," Tom insisted, a bit more intensely than he'd intended.

At this, Jacob smiled a bit himself. "So, you're feeling confident then, based on what you're seeing?"

"I am," the archivist said reassuringly.

"That's very good," the executive replied, nodding again, then appeared to note a new notification that corrupted his brief expression of contentment. "Sorry, Tom, but something's just come up down here. I'll talk to you soon."

"Sure thing, boss," Hallett said and the transmission abruptly ended. "Hang in there, friend," he thought, realizing that Jacob was likely having a similar thought about him if he wasn't already completely engrossed in whatever had occurred back on Earth.

As the Apex approached Venus, Tom could feel the boost to its acceleration and the sensation of the inertial gravity created by the craft's rapid, close approach trickling through his body, even as the ship's artificial system constantly adjusted to compensate for the changes. It was a bit nauseating and he truly began to understand why the gravity couches would be necessary for the sun shot. Compared to Venus, the forces their bodies would be subjected to while slingshotting around the sun would be absolutely astronomical and the archivist already felt as though he could easily collapse to his knees or even all the way to the floor if he took a bad step or his concentration wavered.

Hallett carefully made his way back to the bridge just in time to witness the dramatic view of the planet on its main display, taking up nearly the top half of the wall-sized image. He had known that the ship would reorient itself into an inverted alignment to allow the gravitational force to work against them in a way that was more natural but the maneuver had been so smooth and gradual that he hadn't even felt it.

A few moments later, the image began to shimmer and an alarm sounded.

"We're getting a little atmospheric drag," Briggs announced. For a moment, Sophia looked over at the engineer with concern but simply nodded when he completed his thought. "It's more than we expected but still inside the margin. We're gonna heat up a bit but she can handle it."

"Everyone, brace for a little turbulence," Fields ordered via the crew's implants.

Briggs set his jaw for a moment, then nodded. "We cut it a little too close but the math checks out. Looks like the folks at home are gonna get two shows!"

Outside, the ship's outer surface began to glow with the friction of billions of atmospheric particles being drug along it at an almost-preposterous velocity, which continued to increase despite their cumulative effect.

For a few seconds, the Apex trembled, creaked, and groaned in a decidedly-abnormal fashion until their was a loud bang somewhere along its left side and another, more urgent-sounding alarm erupted from the bridge's speaker system.

"Hull breach! Deck one, left rear!" Briggs yelled over the cacophonous sounds.

Immediately, Steve and Rashid sprang into action, grabbing nanite guns off the wall near the bridge's port-side exit and sprinting down the hall toward the breach.

To his own surprise, Tom was compelled to follow them despite not having been ordered or trained to do so. He managed to catch up just in time to see the two techs launch a series of yellow nanite globs at a long crack that had formed in the corridor's external wall as a geyser-like spray of superheated atmosphere spilled into the passage in front of them.

As Rashid finished sealing the crack, Steve adjusted the dial on his gun to the blue position and half pulled its trigger until the device began emanating a high-pitched whine. He then released its payload, sending the largest sphere of blue nanites the weapon's barrel could accommodate into the air in front of them, which instantly expanded to span the entire hallway, effectively sealing it off with a dark blue, opaque membrane. Beyond it, the doors to the science lab and engineering had automatically sealed, completely containing the toxic atmosphere that had entered through the crack.

"Seal confirmed," Rashid announced to the rest of the crew via his implant.

"Purging section twelve," Briggs replied in a similar fashion as the ship's quaking subsided and the contained area was quickly vented into space before being re-pressurized and filled with the ship's normal atmosphere.

Observed from afar by the eyes of the world, the Apex pulled a fine, glimmering, perfectly-straight thread of matter out from Venus as it accelerated away toward the sun.

CHAPTER 14

THE SUN SHOT

With each passing moment, Tom became increasingly aware that he and the rest of the crew were traveling through space faster than any human beings ever had before. On the view screen at the front of the Apex's bridge, he could literally see the sun, its image filtered to prevent it from being overwhelmingly bright, slowly increasing in size as they hurtled toward it at thousands of kilometers per second.

Astoundingly, the archivist found his mind able to quickly come to terms with that reality, simply staring agape at the image in a profound state of awe until Bob tapped him on the shoulder to get his attention while the rest of the crew began to make their way to the gravity couch bay.

"We're really doing this," Hallett said simply, letting his eyes linger on the screen for a moment longer before turning to face Briggs.

"Like I said before, Mr. Hallett," the engineer confirmed with a nod, "you haven't seen, or felt, anything yet." The older man smiled and motioned for him to follow as he began to make his own way off the bridge.

Immediately, Tom was compelled to comply, more eager than ever to experience the next wondrous aspect of his journey. All at once, the archivist registered a sort of epiphany manifesting in his mind, truly recognizing that he was indeed precisely where he was meant to be. Hallett had experienced fleeting moments of that sort throughout his life, brief surges of certainty so potent that they'd left him reassured for days as to the validity of his existence and his chosen path through it, but he'd never felt anything so strong and prolonged. The sensation persisted, even as they traveled down the lower deck's long, starboard corridor and entered a room, nearly filled to capacity with gravity couches.

For the most part, they all appeared identical, with simple name tags being their only distinguishing characteristic. Still, as Tom approached his capsule-shaped chamber and it opened in response to his proximity, he noted the presence of the single, much-larger variant he'd seen in the science lab back on Earth. Glancing down at its tag, which had apparently been hastily labeled with a marker as opposed to the precise typography of the others, he read the two letters that had been scrawled onto it, "AI," his curiosity piqued.

Throughout all of Jacob's efforts to educate him regarding the particular details of the Nemesis Project and its mission, Tom couldn't recall any mention of any sort of artificial intelligence beyond the limited capacities possessed by the nanites in their various, initialized forms. He therefore stood, somewhat perplexed, attempting to envision what the pod might contain and under what circumstances it might factor into their efforts.

Again, Bob's hand tapped the archivist's shoulder and the engineer spoke up as soon as he'd secured the younger man's attention. "Time to tuck in, Tom. You won't want to be anywhere else for this next part. Trust me."

Briggs grinned knowingly as he completed his statement and Hallett once again felt compelled to immediately comply, recognizing that he had rapidly come to trust Bob and his judgement in a way not dissimilar from the confidence he felt regarding Jacob Westbrook's intentions and decision-making.

To his mild surprise, the inside of the gravity couch was completely devoid of any sort of padding, its surface instead akin to the ship's deck plating despite its contoured shape. As Hallett climbed inside and laid himself along its length, he felt its cold, unyielding form through his clothing for a moment but the sensation was quickly replaced by a feeling of perfect, warm comfort as nanite tendrils erupted from the tiny holes beneath him and lifted his body a few inches into the air. They then surrounded and began carefully cradling it with precisely the correct amount of force at every point of contact to trigger an almost-immediate state of total relaxation.

Seeing the expected, simultaneously shocked and soothed expression on the archivist's face, the engineer nodded and quickly closed the device's lid.

For a moment, Tom felt a little rush of panic at being sealed in such an enclosed, absolutely-darkened space but before he could react to that instinct, there was a tiny jab in his neck and the archivist immediately felt himself go completely limp, unable to move at all despite remaining fully conscious. At that moment, a slew of diagnostic information was pushed into his augmented vision, indicating that the gravity couch was functioning as intended and that he had been properly sealed and secured within it.

Tom was further reassured to hear Sophia's calm, measured voice in his mind via his implant, and could distinctly sense the presence of the other crew members as they entered their pods, the chambers clearly having been linked and preprogrammed to facilitate such interactions to help comfort their occupants when in use. "All couches occupied and secure," the commander confirmed as Bob joined the group, having delayed his own entry to ensure that all the other units were functioning perfectly. "Engaging overdrive burn in three... two... one..."

If he'd been able to, Tom might have tensed up during Sophia's countdown. If so, he likely would have pulled a muscle somewhere in his body when the shocking force produced by the Apex's main engines hit it, boosting to their absolute limit to quickly attain the remaining velocity required to perform a close, rapid orbit of the sun.

For the most part, the gravity couch did its job, holding Tom generally in place even as the millions of nanites surrounding him constantly adjusted to absorb, negate, and push against the external forces being applied to his body. It was a delicate balancing act specifically designed to keep him alive and well throughout the ship's extreme maneuver, which otherwise certainly would have killed him and everyone else aboard it. Still, the archivist could feel his innards being smashed, contorted, and otherwise traumatized in a way that he couldn't help worrying about despite the pain of the experience having largely been numbed by whatever had been injected into his neck.

Outside, the Apex's surface glowed even more brightly and intensely than it had while skimming the Veneutian atmosphere. This gave the ship the appearance of a scintillating projectile or a pulse of pure energy as it rounded the sun in a matter of minutes and exited away from it with astounding speed and force, depositing a trail of incidentally-collected, stellar matter behind it that was observed as an uneven chain of shimmering pearls, which quickly dissipated into the surrounding void.

"Godspeed," Jacob Westbrook repeated under his breath, observing the phenomenon from mission control and despite understanding that it had actually occurred several minutes before he'd been able to witness it.

CHAPTER 15

DECELERATION

For a time, Tom Hallett simply hung within his gravity couch in a sort of limbo state, barely able to process what he'd experienced. He wasn't entirely certain if that had purely been a result of the sun shot itself, the drugs he'd been given, or a combination of the two but as he once again became aware of Sophia Fields' voice in his mind, the archivist realized that he had no idea how much time had actually passed since he'd entered his pod and the maneuver had begun. It was then that he also became aware that the craft's main engines had cut out at some point, the thrust they could provide clearly being inconsequential relative to the star's gravitational effect. "Peak velocity attained. No obstacles detected. Everybody catch your breath for a few minutes."

Tom did his best to comply but quickly recognized that the commander's statement had been metaphorical, still unable to will any portion of his body into action through any amount of conscious thought. He of course knew that everyone else on the ship was going through exactly the same thing in their respective gravity couches, which was somewhat comforting, but it still took Hallett several minutes to properly calm his mind and come completely back to his senses. As a result, his first coherent thought was a simple realization that he would likely never experience anything more intense than what his body had just been put through and live to tell of it.

As if in response, Sophia's voice returned with another of its straightforward, calm instructions. "Approaching nav point gamma. Prepare for deceleration."

Slowly, Tom became aware of a slight change in his orientation. It was extremely subtle and he might not have noticed it at all if not for Fields' announcement but he nonetheless became aware that he was gradually turning upside down as a result of the ship doing the same while it flipped a hundred and eighty degrees to point its main engines toward the anomaly and its nose back at the rapidly-shrinking sun, still careening through space at a significant portion of the speed of light.

When the rotation completed, Sophia's voice returned to deliver a simple, business-like countdown. "Beginning deceleration in three... two... one..."

The Apex trembled and rumbled as a whole when the main engines reignited but the resulting force applied to Tom's body felt almost tame and gentle by comparison to the sun shot. Still, he could somehow sense that the forces at play were significant and that they likely would have been sufficient to knock him on his ass had he not remained in his protective cocoon.

After several minutes of an almost eerie lack of new information, a chime sounded in Hallett's mind and Sophia's voice confirmed its purpose. "Stable deceleration vector achieved. Disengaging gravity couches."

A moment later, Tom felt another prick in his neck and almost immediately found himself able to exert force against the nanites holding him in place, which quickly retreated into their holes and disappeared as the device's lid opened and his body came to rest on its cold, hard lower half.

The archivist quickly sat up and effectively leapt out of the pod, grabbing its side just in time to prevent himself from flying toward the room's ceiling in the almost non-existent natural gravity.

Tom's head swirled and he felt almost overwhelmingly nauseous, worried that he might reflexively wretch.

"Easy, Mr. Hallett," Bob offered, sitting on the edge of his own container and slowly lowering his feet to the floor, where they were met by a cluster of deck plate nanites and temporarily affixed to it. "Give yourself a minute to adjust to it. We are upside down after all, at least as far as your brain's concerned."

"Right," Tom acknowledged, continuing to grip the side of his gravity couch until his head began to clear and he managed to slowly bring his feet and legs down to the ground and reorient himself.

"Well done, sir," Briggs said sincerely. "You really do have a great set of space legs. No doubt about it."

"Thanks, Bob," Hallett acknowledged, looking around the room and noting that a few of the other crew members, including Major Pryce, had brought hands up to their mouths, likely concerned about possible eruptions from themselves despite none being produced.

"So, how long is it going to take us to slow down?" Tom asked, returning his attention to Briggs and noting that the ship's engines were continuing to operate at a high level, albeit not as intensely as they had been during the overdrive burn.

The older man rolled his eyes and head up a moment, then looked back at Hallett. "About five hours, give or take. That'll get us close enough to make more meaningful observations, collect some samples, and slow us down enough so we don't just plow into the damn thing before we figure out what to do about it..." The engineer paused for a moment, then added "...hopefully."

At this, Tom couldn't help giving Bob a somewhat-worried look.

"To be honest, Mr. Hallett, we're about to enter uncharted territory here. Everything we've done up to this point has been at least theorized for quite a long time. Not that it was trivial by any means, mind you, but we had a pretty good idea what to expect. From here on out, things are almost certainly going to get a bit... fuzzier."

The archivist nodded. "I see."

"Truth is," the engineer concluded, "we're probably gonna end up shooting from the hip quite a bit for the rest of this sleigh ride, so apologies in advance if my answers to your questions get a little less... reliable."

"I understand, Bob," Tom said reassuringly, then quickly added, "I'm sure they'll be great. They certainly have been so far."

The older man shrugged in a sort of "aw shucks, just doing my job" gesture and Hallett once again found himself unable to imagine anyone better suited to the role he'd been assigned.

Gradually, activity on the Apex returned to what Tom supposed he'd refer to as "normal" if he did indeed get the opportunity to describe the events he was experiencing to anyone in the future. With that thought in mind and the rest of the crew busy at their various stations, the archivist retreated to the crew quarters and spent much of the time during the deceleration burn writing down his thoughts and observations in an old, paper journal with an antique, silver pen that had been passed down through generations of his family. As it glided along the pages, the heavy but perfectly-balanced writing implement slightly tingled in Hallet's hand with a sort of intangible magic as it always seemed to when he held it firmly and his best words began to flow from it.

CHAPTER 16

BREAKDOWN

As the deceleration burn neared its end, everyone aboard the Apex was summoned to the bridge and Tom made his way down from the quiet corner he'd found in the crew quarters, arriving just ahead of Robert Briggs and the two, active technicians who'd been assisting him in engineering.

With the entire group gathered, Sophia Fields looked around to ensure she had their full attention, then nodded. "Okay, let's get a better look at what we're dealing with."

As if in response, the ship's main engines cut out and the chamber fell almost completely silent while simple, maneuvering thrusters worked to rotate the Apex back toward the anomaly, the bridge's main display showing a sweeping star field as the distant sun fell away out of view.

Soon after, the ever-expanding edge of the phenomenon appeared, rippling like an irregular wave of energy out from a glowing, swirling mass of completely alien-looking matter.

Again, the archivist felt a slight sense of nausea as the reorientation completed but he mostly disregarded it, utterly stunned by the terrifying magnificence that nearly filled the screen before him. "How big is it?" Hallett wondered aloud, not necessarily expecting an answer.

"About eighty percent of Earth's volume at the moment," Briggs offered. "And yes," the engineer elaborated, anticipating Tom's next question, "it will be significantly larger by the time we reach it."

The archivist didn't doubt that, clearly able to observe the structure's growth even from what he imagined must still be a significant distance. "How much time do we have before..."

The older man cut him off, raising his hands in a palms-up gesture of uncertainty. "Before it fries us? A few hours at our current velocity.

Of course, we can slow down, or even stop and head back toward home at this point pretty easily, assuming that we have enough warning that is."

Hallett nodded but kept his gaze firmly on the display, almost hypnotized by its scintillating, seemingly-rhythmic movements, until it was replaced by a view of Jacob Westbrook standing in mission control.

Without delay, the executive spoke, immediately gaining the attention of everyone present. "Congratulations on your arrival, Apex. We show you in proximity to the anomaly with course and speed as planned. As you know, there will be a significant communication delay at this distance, so I've sent this message a bit in advance to coincide with the completion of your reorientation maneuver." The image and audio began to break up a bit but seemed to clear as the big man continued. "I know the task before you may seem more daunting than ever but rest assured, we will continue to do everything we can to assist you and remain confident..."

Tom's heart sank as the transmission abruptly cut off, then seemed to pause in his chest as a new notification appeared in his augmented vision. "Communication Error: No other implants detected. Would you like to disable further notifications and reestablish communication when a network becomes available?"

"Yes," the archivist carefully thought, doing his best not to panic as he looked around the room, seeing similarly befuddled and annoyed expressions on the faces of everyone else present. Indeed, they had apparently not only been cut off from mission control back on Earth, but from each other as well.

Immediately, Sophia moved from her position at the center of the bridge and came to stand next to Bob, studying his engineering console as he manipulated several controls and shook his head slightly. "It's worse than we thought?" Fields asked, examining the results of his efforts herself.

"Yeah," Briggs acknowledged. "Some sort of electromagnetic interference but it's a bit... shifted somehow. I can't explain it... yet."

The commander nodded. "Are we in any danger from it?"

"I don't think so," the engineer said quickly but not definitively. "The nannies seem to be filtering out most of it but clearly, not enough. Dr. Clay could probably say for sure what if any effect it might have on us."

"I'll need a couple volunteers for some tests in medical," the physician offered, inserting herself into the conversation at the mention of her name.

Immediately, Rashid and Steve stepped forward. "Right here, doc," Steve said confidently as if to punctuate and confirm their collective action.

"Excellent," Clay replied, motioning for them to follow her to the ship's medical facility.

"Any chance we can get our comms back?" Fields asked, turning her attention back to the engineer.

"Maybe, if I can figure out why these readings are so... off," Briggs responded, continuing to study his display and work controls.

"Stick with it, Bob, and keep a running calculation for the burn we'd have to execute to get back out into clear space if necessary."

"Yes, commander," the engineer said dutifully, "but keep in mind that we're still moving like a bat out of Hell. Even if we hit the brakes right now, it'd take a while to get back beyond the point where we lost comms with the thrust we can generate, even with a full burn."

"Understood," Sophia acknowledged, then turned to face the rest of the crew. "Okay, everybody. We knew something like this was a possibility, so nothing's really changed. Proceed as planned and use the hardwired comm panels to stay in touch. Dismissed."

With that, the remaining crew members nodded and returned to their respective stations, Tom following Monique Maxwell back toward the science lab after she made a subtle gesture toward him.

As they entered the port-side corridor from the bridge, Maxwell spoke to the archivist directly. "Sorry to draft you, Mr. Hallett, but I could use a little help monitoring a few instruments with my implant down and the techs otherwise occupied if you don't mind."

"Not at all, Dr. Maxwell," Tom said almost casually. "Just tell me what you need."

CHAPTER 17

ERUPTION

The Apex's science lab contained an expectedly-impressive array of equipment and monitoring stations, their purposes admittedly far beyond Tom's understanding and experience for the most part. Still, after a few, calm and specific instructions from Maxwell, the archivist felt reasonably confident taking up a position at one of the stations and observing the indicators he'd been assigned to watch for changes beyond a given threshold.

Meanwhile, Monique moved about the room, interacting with and assessing various other devices and occasionally asking Hallett to call out the values he was observing.

Eventually, the scientist seemed to exhaust her options, reverting to a state similar to the one he'd found her in when Jacob had introduced them while she waited for the results of her efforts to be presented.

Noting the scientist's perplexed, worried expression, Tom took the opportunity to speak, hoping to provide assistance beyond his meager contributions to that point. "Not seeing what you expected?"

"Yes and no," Maxwell said simply, keeping her eyes on her equipment. "Most of these readings are exactly what we imagined we'd encounter beyond the distortions generated by the emissions but there's something else. I can see why Bob is scratching his head. Some of this just doesn't make any sense."

Before Hallett could formulate another question, an alarm went off and Monique tensed up, moving toward her console and furiously working its controls. "Get on that comm panel and open a line to the bridge, would you, Tom?"

"Sure thing," the archivist replied, making his way over to the wall panel and tapping a few simple, intuitive buttons until a soft chime signaled that the connection had been established.

"Commander, we have a mass ejection in progress! Be advised that it's headed straight for us!" Maxwell reported.

"Can we navigate around it?" Fields asked.

"Negative," the scientist replied after consulting her instruments. "We're too close and it's too large. Estimated impact in... two minutes and thirty-two seconds!"

"Understood," Sophia acknowledged. "Mr. Pryce, kindly remove that object from our path." Field said this in her customarily calm and confident voice but Tom could tell, even through the imperfect replication of the comm system's speaker, that there was a hint of panic and worry in it.

"Right away, commander," the tactical officer affirmed.

Monique worked a new set of controls, applying a zoom and filtering effect to the image of the anomaly on the lab's main display that allowed them to clearly see the enormous, undulating mass of glowing, liquified matter that had been hurled out of it toward them at a preposterous speed.

A moment later, the ship's weapon systems began to fire, sending the reverberating sounds of massive energy build ups and discharges throughout its length as volleys of red nanites from a single, central cannon and shots from two, enormous, adjacent railguns embedded in the ship's dorsal section were fired toward the incoming threat.

Being much faster, the railgun discharges reached their target first, instantly penetrating the mass and passing through it like needles through cloth but leaving it largely intact and otherwise undisturbed.

"Negligible impact from the railguns, commander," Pryce reported. "Preparing another volley of nanites, just in case."

"Understood," Fields acknowledged, then triggered a ship-wide announcement through the hardwired comm system. "Everyone, get to your gravity couches. We may need to ride this one out!"

Maxwell looked at her display a moment longer, her eyes widening as the volley of nanites slammed into the approaching mass and a new set of readings appeared. "Oh, no. That's not good," she said in a surprisingly-reserved voice, then cried out, "Pryce! Hold your fire!" just as the second volley was released.

"No!" The scientist exclaimed and for a moment, there was silence.

"Sorry, doc, but it looks like it's dissipating," Pryce offered.

"Negative," Monique corrected, clearly annoyed by the soldier's decision to fire again so quickly. "It's reacting... superheating beyond the visual spectrum, but it's not dissipating! We're going to be in serious trouble if that second group accelerates the reaction!"

"Son of a..." Pryce began but Sophia cut him off. "Everyone to the grav couch bay, now!"

"They won't be enough," Maxwell muttered under her breath but nonetheless moved to exit the lab, motioning for Tom to follow her.

Inside the gravity couch chamber, Rashid and Steve were already applying coats of blue nanites to its front wall.

"You read my mind, fellas," Monique acknowledged, retrieving a nanite gun of her own from the wall near the starboard door and assisting the effort as the rest of the crew arrived and began making their way to their pods.

"Will that be enough shielding?" Sophia asked, putting a hand on the last gun in the rack.

"It's gonna have to be," Maxwell said somewhat doubtfully. "We're almost out of time. Okay, everyone tuck in! We've got less than thirty seconds!"

The rest of the crew complied apart from Steve and Rashid, who continued applying layers of blue nanites to the surrounding walls.

"Now, gentlemen!" Fields ordered as she closed the lid of her pod.

"On our way, commander," Rashid acknowledged, backing toward his couch as he continued to fire the gun until it ran dry.

Meanwhile, Steve made his way over to the rack and replaced his depleted rifle to begin the automated reloading process before grabbing the other weapon and twisting its dial to the blue position.

"Come on, Steve!" Rashid pleaded, sensing what his friend was likely about to do.

"It's not gonna be enough," the huskier of the two techs said, firing the gun at the wall.

Rashid set his jaw, then climbed back out of his open pod. "Fine! We'll do it together." He tried to make his way to the rack but Cox intercepted him, grabbing the senior tech with one hand and pushing him back into the pod as he continued to fire with the other.

"No!" Rashid screamed as Steve thrust him into place and slammed the lid closed just as the Apex plunged into the leading edge of the burning mass.

From inside his sealed gravity couch, Tom could hear the faint sounds of Steven Cox's nanite gun continuing to fire as the young man began to howl in a mixture of defiant anger and pain. Simultaneously, the archivist's mind was flooded with its own slew of pain responses as lesions began to form and widen at various points along the surface of his paralyzed body. "No!" Hallett tried to scream as he realized that he was being burned alive by the intense radiation emanating from the mass they were traveling through.

CHAPTER 18

BLACK STAR

If the mass had been much larger or Steve had failed to apply the last few layers of nanites, they all surely would have died right then and there. As it turned out, the young technician's efforts had been just enough to prevent fatal exposure for everyone in the gravity couches.

Still, the crew exited their protective cocoons carefully and gingerly, their flesh oozing and burning in a variety of places. Dr. Clay, whose left hand had been particularly savaged by the incident, nonetheless immediately leapt to Steve's fallen form, briefly assessing his charred remains before concluding that he was beyond the point of saving. "Everyone, get to medical. I need to administer radiation therapy right now or we're all going to drop!"

The other crew members complied, staggering their way toward the adjacent medical bay like the walking dead behind the doctor, who willed herself into the lead despite her own suffering. At the rear of the group, Fields and Pryce leaned on each other for support, both of their faces marred by dripping, oozing wounds that appeared more significant than those of the others if only as a result of their locations.

As soon as everyone had entered the medical facility, Clay tapped a series of controls and the doors sealed while a cloud of green nanites was injected into the air all around them.

Immediately, Tom could feel a tingling all throughout his body as the faintly-glowing mist surrounded him and his wounds began to close. Slowly, his pain and nausea faded and he soon found himself feeling almost normal despite the odd sensations rippling through him like chills as the tiny robots completed their work and exited him, falling to the floor in a fine shower like talcum powder.

For the most part, everyone seemed to have recovered or at least responded positively to the treatment but the archivist noted that Pryce continued to hold his head as if he were still in pain despite the wounds having disappeared from his face.

"We need to treat the backup crew in their pods," Clay said, examining her own, repaired hands, then lowered her head, specifically looking away from Rashid and at Sophia, "and activate one of the techs."

The commander nodded, making her way over to the room's rifle rack and removing a nanite gun from it as she adjusted it to its active, green setting.

Within a minute, the crew had made their way back to the gravity couch chamber, only pausing for a moment to allow Clay time to cover Steve with a sheet. They then inserted their rifle barrels into injection ports at the bases of the couches containing their respective backups and delivered a dose of green nanites into their pods.

Rashid did this for both the sleeping technicians, then woke one of them, Mikaela Hellevic, quietly informing her of what had happened to Steve.

"I'm so sorry, Rashid," she said softly. "I wanted to help, but not like this."

The older tech nodded but said nothing, making his way to Bob as if seeking instruction.

The engineer put a hand on Rashid's shoulder and leaned in, whispering something into his ear and the younger man nodded again, motioning for Mikaela to follow him as he slowly but purposefully exited the room.

Briggs then made his way over to one of the chamber's control consoles and pulled up one of his engineering screens.

"What's the damage, Bob?" Sophia asked, moving to join him.

"Outer hull's severely compromised. The nannies are keeping the barrier tanks intact, just barely, but we need to initiate the repair protocol now or we're gonna lose most of what we've got left real quick."

"Do it," Fields ordered.

"Done," the engineer confirmed. All around them, the ship began to resonate and hum as trillions of yellow nanites simultaneously activated and began working to repair its outer hull.

"Estimated time to repair... about twenty-three minutes for one hundred percent recovery," Briggs concluded.

"Anything else we need to worry about?" Sophia asked, seeing the look of concern on Bob's face.

"The environmental system is almost redlining and we lost the green room. I'd recommend keeping it sealed as the organic remains are saturated. It's not worth the resources to try to purge it at this point." Briggs paused for a moment, setting his jaw. "We're gonna be okay but we won't survive another one of those."

He paused again and Sophia prodded, knowing whatever he was reluctant to say was likely important. "What is it, Bob?"

The engineer turned to face her, his expression completely dour and serious. "Whatever we're going to do, we'll need to do it soon if we want to make it home. We can maintain the original mission parameters for a bit longer as is but at a certain point, this may turn into a one-way trip, depending on what we end up having to do."

"Understood," Fields acknowledged. "Keep me posted, Bob."

"Will do," the engineer said somberly, returning his gaze to his instruments.

"Any progress on restoring comms?" Sophia asked, seemingly eager to change the subject.

Briggs shook his head. "The soup's thicker than ever out there and it's only gonna get worse. I think we're too deep into it to cut through. I might be able to get our local network back with some tweaks to the filters but it'll take some time to suss it out."

"So, we're officially cut off?" Fields asked as a matter of formality.

"I'd say yes at this point, barring some sort of epiphany," Bob confirmed.

"Understood," Sophia said softly. "Do what you can with comms but obviously, concentrate on keeping us alive and in one piece."

"Sure thing, commander," Briggs acknowledged, continuing to scan through the ship's various status and damage reports.

Apparently satisfied, Sophia made her way over to the single, large gravity couch that towered over the others in the room, checking its logs to ensure that it had automatically made use of its own supply of nanites, which she knew accounted for at least some of its additional size and complexity beyond that of the devices surrounding it. She then moved to its latch and pulled on it, opening the chamber as Tom observed her with rapt curiosity.

From within the pod's spacious confines, a large, suited, grey-haired gentleman rose up and immediately moved to extricate himself, confidently and precisely placing his immaculately-polished, black dress shoes on the deck plating and rising up atop them in a manner indicating that he was completely comfortable in the ship's gravity.

The man was impressively large, both in height and girth, his perfectly tailored suit minimizing certain aspects of his form while accentuating others to an almost-magical degree. To a person, everyone in the room immediately took note, providing him their full attention without any prompting.

As the big man scanned the room, clearly noting those around him in a less awestruck and more analytical fashion, Hallett's eyes at last focused on his lapel pin, which projected a single, shimmering, black star, still visible in his augmented vision despite his implant's crippled state.

For a moment, Tom felt a lump in his throat as if his heart were trying to climb up and out of his chest, realizing that he was indeed standing in the presence of the most-powerful man in the world.

CHAPTER 19

TERMINATION

It had been several hours since they'd lost their ability to communicate with the Apex but Jacob Westbrook found himself surprisingly calm. He supposed he had good reasons for that, still able to view the ship's progress toward its destination thanks to the coordinated efforts of several, orbital telescopes. Moreover, he'd successfully averted the public demotion of his company's most-senior, class two executive through a series of careful and deftly-executed efforts behind the scenes.

In truth, that was one of the main reasons why he'd never actively sought promotion beyond his current station, understanding that the differences between the two ranks were more a matter of prestige and potential exposure than actual power. Indeed, class three was his wheelhouse, his comfort zone, the place where he felt most at home and confident and he had no doubt that the man above him, whose career and legacy if nothing else had been saved by his actions, would undoubtedly concur, continuing to eagerly support him and his initiatives moving forward as he always had.

Beyond that, Jacob knew that he had not one but two aces in the hole. Not only was his boss, the man he trusted and respected more than anyone else in the world, aboard the ship, having no doubt been awakened shortly after it had become apparent that communication with mission control was unlikely to be restored, but Tom Hallett as well.

He had only known the archivist for a short time but Westbrook somehow understood at the core of his being that the young man was destined to play an important part in what was unfolding. In fact, he'd already done so, literally saving his life as he'd lain dying on the ground outside a pod a few days prior but the executive was certain there was more to it and had been profoundly relieved when his new friend had agreed to accept the obviously-perilous assignment to the ship's crew. Still, there was a selfish part of Jacob that had been reluctant to send him away, feeling soothed and comforted by the younger man's presence in a way that was almost completely foreign to him. He reasoned at least part of that had been born from the circumstances of their initial meeting but again, Jacob couldn't help feeling there was more to it. When he boiled it down in his mind, he found himself forced to conclude that Tom Hallett felt less like a friend to him and more like a companion, a counterpart that he somehow felt less complete without. That was a particularly-inconvenient realization given everything that was happening but Westbrook willed himself to acknowledge and confront it, knowing from painful experience that ignoring such thoughts would not end well for him or anyone concerned.

With all this percolating in his mind, the executive stared out of his private pod's window as the vehicle approached the Pryce building. It was a particularly-ancient structure compared to others in the area but it had been built to last and remained a formidable presence in the city's skyline, projecting a potent air of utility and pragmatism amid the more sleek, shapely, and modern buildings that surrounded it. Indeed, to Westbrook's eye, only his own company's headquarters was more impressive in the focused, singular vision of its design.

As had become the case everywhere, the area outside the building was filled with people, the world having largely ground to a halt and its citizens taking to the streets for a variety of reasons as they impatiently waited to learn their fate.

For the most part, this had amounted to little more than an inconvenience in the region but Jacob was well aware that other parts of the country, and the world at large, were experiencing significantly more turmoil. He was therefore relieved and grateful that he was still able to move about the city if in a somewhat-delayed fashion, allowing him to visit the Pryce Foundation in person to observe the progress they'd made analyzing the fields that were disrupting their communication systems.

After being cleared through a security checkpoint, his pod made its way into a small entrance adjacent to the building's underground parking garage. As it automatically opened before him, Westbrook's vehicle was granted access to the private area within a sub-basement that Conrad Pryce himself had once used for his own comings and goings.

The pod's door automatically opened as it glided to a stop and Jacob immediately stepped out of it, the penetrating clacks of his heels echoing off the chamber's concrete surfaces as he approached another suited gentleman. To his surprise, he noted that Bryan Davenport, the Pryce Foundation's lone three-star executive and the man who'd invited him, had come to greet him in person, opting not to send a drone or underling to act as an escort.

"Good afternoon, Mr. Westbrook. It's a pleasure to see you again," the younger man said smoothly and Jacob responded in kind, giving him a quick but firm handshake and a nod before following him toward a private elevator in an adjacent, dimly-lit room.

Jacob had encountered Davenport a few times during his rapid ascent through the executive ranks. Just a few years prior, he'd first met Bryan, then an eager class twelve, attempting to make his mark as the newly-appointed head of an obscure research facility. A year later, he did just that with an unprecedented jump to rank six as a result of a series of unexpected innovations that had proven vital to the Nemesis Project's efforts. From there, his promotion to class three, the youngest to ever achieve the rank at just shy of forty, had by then seemed almost unsurprising and inevitable. In short, Bryan Davenport was as formidable and ambitious as they came, which simultaneously impressed and concerned Westbrook. Indeed, the big man couldn't help wondering if he'd perhaps been promoted a bit too quickly and aggressively by the Pryce Foundation's board, confident that his own employer would have been at least a bit more conservative with such praise.

Nonetheless, Jacob felt comfortable enough in his company, having gotten to know Davenport a bit via their previous interactions and ultimately concluding that he was simply an exceptionally-focused and driven man, who preferred to dispense with pleasantries and niceties in favor of progress whenever possible. This was reflected in his attire, which had an almost basic, utilitarian quality to it, despite being finely made and fitted, particularly when compared with Westbrook's decidedly striking, elaborate appearance. More than anything, it was that confident conclusion regarding Davenport's nature that made his decision to take the time to greet him in person somewhat perplexing and noteworthy.

Consequently, Jacob's confusion was further exacerbated when after their short, silent elevator ride, the younger man led him to a large, vacant conference room just a few steps away that was capable of seating dozens around an enormous but elegant, wooden table, only to lock the door behind them. He then gestured for Westbrook to take a seat before making his way to a cabinet at the room's far end.

As was typical of the Pryce building's facilities, the meeting area was both impressive and practical, the table and its surrounding, leather chairs efficiently and cleverly lit from above by strategically-placed, indirect fixtures concealed in its ceiling. This allowed the display along its far wall, which featured a collection of firearms representing the evolution of that invention throughout history, to stand out prominently via its own, slightly-more-intense illumination. The presented weapons began with a simple musket and culminated with one of the nanite guns currently being used aboard the Apex, with several noteworthy innovations represented between them via various, pristine examples.

As Jacob settled into his chair, Davenport retrieved a bottle, two shot glasses, and a small, metal box from the cabinet, then made his way over to the table, depositing the items on it before taking the seat next to Westbrook. He opened the bottle and immediately began to pour a significant quantity of the dark liquor into one of the shot glasses. "Care to join me?" The younger executive asked this, keeping his eyes on the glass as he finished the pour.

"It's a bit early for me," Westbrook stated matter of factly, never having been much of a drinker despite possessing a significant tolerance for alcohol as a person of size.

"Oh, come on, Jacob. We should celebrate," Davenport prodded.

At this, Westbrook raised an eyebrow, truly baffled by the younger man's unorthodox behavior. "What are we celebrating, Bryan?"

"Why, your success of course," Davenport replied immediately.

The big man put up a hand. "I believe that's a bit premature, Mr. Davenport."

"Nonsense," Bryan insisted, then looked at the older executive somewhat incredulously. "Surely, you must realize the position you're in by now?"

Westbrook set his jaw and pondered, not really comprehending what Davenport was inferring.

"Unbelievable," the younger man said, picking up the nearly-full glass and taking a big swig to consume nearly half of its contents in a single gulp before decisively replacing it on the table with a thud. "You really don't get it, do you?"

Not feeling as though he should, Jacob simply shrugged and shook his head.

"You're about to become the new king of the world, Westbrook, assuming that any of us survive to be your subjects." Bryan laughed for a moment, then looked down at his drink, seemingly not quite ready to finish it. "The whole planet is watching the show you're putting on, Jacob, and when this is all over, you're gonna have a blank check. You do get that, right?"

Westbrook shook his head a bit more vehemently, at last understanding what Bryan had been so uncharacteristically vaguely conveying. "I just did my job," he said simply.

Davenport laughed again, then picked up his glass and finished his drink with another big gulp. "That's what's so infuriating about you," the younger man admitted. "I've been chasing you my whole career and now, you're gonna blow past me again in a way I'll never be able to match, much less exceed, and you don't even give a fuck. To you, it's just business as usual."

Jacob's mouth hung open slightly, immediately recognizing the pure, wounded tone in the younger man's voice and simultaneously realizing that he had never even considered the possibility of such a reaction. To him, the things he'd done since the inception of the Nemesis Project had been so vital, so unquestionably necessary, that he had simply done them, never once contemplating the effect they might have on his career or the ambitions of others. Completely flabbergasted, he somberly said, "I'm sorry, Bryan."

"Of course you are," Davenport replied, then shook his own head, seemingly trying to clear it. "Anyway, I've got something to show you."

Westbrook glanced down at the little, black box on the table, a single, obvious, grey switch on its side.

The younger man nodded, placing a hand on it but purposefully keeping his thumb away from the switch as he spoke. "We've analyzed the readings the Apex managed to transmit leading up to the communication breakdown. It's quite the cocktail, something that'd never naturally occur outside of that hell hole, but we managed to recreate it, or something close to it anyway."

Bryan extended his thumb and flipped the switch.

Instantly, Jacob's implant went offline, everything but its tiny "No signal" indicator disappearing in his augmented vision. "So, they can't communicate with each other either," Westbrook noted, a frown forming on his face.

"Bingo," Davenport confirmed. "Well, not with their implants anyway."

"Is there any way to cut through it?" Jacob asked.

The younger man shook his head. "The emissions are extremely strong and they saturate just about every known band. The only way to stop it is at the source and even then, the field takes a little while to dissipate."

"What's the range on that thing?" Jacob asked, pointing to the pocket-sized box.

"A couple meters, and we had to use a hydrogen cell to get that. The anomaly must contain an absurd amount of energy to produce a field large enough to affect the ship at the range where they lost comms. The good news is, no one on Earth could generate enough juice to reproduce this at a meaningful scale for long, so our networks should be safe from widespread tampering for the most part, even if someone else figures out the how of it."

"That's something," Westbrook acknowledged when Davenport stood, collecting the bottle and glasses as he moved to return them to the cabinet. Seeing this, Jacob leaned forward and picked up the little device from the table with both hands, eager to disable it and reestablish his connection to the network as quickly as possible.

When the big man's thumb flipped the switch, he cried out involuntarily as a surge of electrical current passed into his hands from the box's surfaces and delivered an intense, prolonged shock to his system. Immediately, his feet and legs reflexively kicked out under the table and he pitched back in his chair, unable to release his grip on the device. "No!" Jacob screamed, his entire body shaking violently for several more seconds until the current abated, his arms fell limp at his sides, and the box came to rest in his lap as his head slumped forward.

At this, Davenport smiled, closing the cabinet after replacing the items and slowly making his way back over to Westbrook, the big man faintly wheezing as a measure of saliva trickled out of his lowered, open mouth and onto his tie.

"A drooling idiot. That truly does sum you up nicely, Mr. Westbrook," Bryan observed, reaching down and pressing a lever on the chair's back to lower it into a partially-reclined position before pulling it away from the table and rotating it until the stunned executive's inert feet and legs were drug out into the open and left mostly facing the wall of guns. He then grabbed the sides of Jacob's skull and eased it back onto the headrest, looking down into his wide, terrified eyes. "You know, if it wasn't for the mess it'd make, I'd smash this fat head of yours in against that table a few times to finish you off for good, you oblivious prick."

The older man moaned in a seemingly vaguely-conscious state, his eyes and jaw slightly quivering but the rest of him remaining completely still.

"Sorry, Jake," Davenport said insincerely. "That jolt was supposed to knock you out cold but I guess there's a bit too much of you for that these days, isn't there, your highness?" He reached down again, giving Westbrook's belly a few, disrespectful pats and a quick rub before grabbing the box from his lap and sliding it into the big man's inner suit jacket pocket, careful not to trigger its switch. "For what it's worth, I would have set this thing up to kill you outright if I could have but most of the cell's power has to go to keeping that pesky implant of yours offline. You'll note that it's completely unaware of your condition and unable to help you recover. A nice, little side effect, wouldn't you agree?"

The incapacitated executive let out a louder moan, clearly trying but unable to speak.

"I know. I know," Bryan said soothingly. "It probably hurts like a son of a bitch. You really should've had that drink with me, Jacob. It would have made things so much easier for both of us. Still, I do have to admit," he continued as he moved to Westbrook's feet, grabbing his ankles through their splendid socks and pulling him off the chair until it rolled away and he was left flat on his back on the floor. "It is rather satisfying, finally getting to watch you struggle for a change, your majesty."

Davenport released his grip, letting the big man's fancy shoes drop to the ground where they jittered for a few seconds before falling still on the room's carpet while he helplessly gasped for air, the dead weight of his bulky chest fully pressing down on his weakened lungs. "That really is a spectacular outfit, sire," Bryan acknowledged, looking Westbrook over from head to toe and clearly relishing the older man's obvious distress. "Too bad no one who gives a shit is ever gonna see you again, or get the chance to kiss your ring, or your ass, or any other part of you for that matter," he concluded, kicking the leather sole of Jacob's motionless, left shoe and grinning when the executive's foot took more than a full second to briefly shudder in response.

At this, Westbrook moaned for a third time, more loudly than ever, at last managing to call out, "Please! Someone! Help me!"

Bryan shook his head. "Don't waste your breath, big fella. These rooms are all completely soundproofed. Allow me to demonstrate." He walked over to the display wall, pulled an antique revolver off of it and opened its cylinder. Davenport then reached into his own suit jacket pocket and removed two bullets from it with his free hand, quickly slotting them into the first two chambers before snapping it closed as he slowly walked back toward Westbrook. "Don't worry Jacob. It'll all be over soon. I promise," he said, examining the gun to ensure that it was properly loaded and ready to fire before returning his attention to his victim.

To the younger man's surprise, he found that the older executive had managed to get himself into a half-seated position, palming the carpet and pressing his elbows into it as he desperately tried to lift himself the rest of the way off the ground, his feet once again waggling almost comically as he simultaneously tried to will his reluctant legs into action.

Seeing Davenport's approach, the big man extended a hand toward him in an instinctive, defensive gesture, barely managing to hold himself in place as he simply asked, "Why?"

Bryan laughed, shaking his head. "Because, Mr. Westbrook, I'll never get another chance to make you disappear. By the way, did you know this building has an incinerator?"

"No!" Jacob cried out as the man above him took aim.

A second later, Davenport fired twice, hitting the big man first in the gut, then in the center of his chest.

For a moment, Westbrook simply stared up at his killer, his mouth hanging agape as he realized that the bullet fired through his abdomen had embedded in his spine. He looked down at his involuntarily twitching feet, noting that he could no longer feel them or anything below his midsection, then collapsed back to the carpet, unconscious, as blood began to ooze from his wounds, soaking into the various layers of his suit, which prevented any of it from spilling onto the surrounding floor. Above him, Bryan extracted a handkerchief from his right-front trouser pocket and began wiping the pistol as he moved to replace it on the wall.

Davenport then walked to Westbrook's chair, resetting its back and returning it to its normal position at the conference table. Below him, the big man's extremities continued to softly quiver but he found himself surprisingly unconcerned, knowing that Westbrook was at best in no condition to resist him and would soon be a pile of ash in the building's basement regardless of his current state. He therefore confidently moved to grab Jacob's wrists, rehearsing in his mind the responses he'd give if he were ever questioned about the executive's disappearance as he began to drag him toward the room's only exit.

"Why, yes," he thought. "Mr. Westbrook did come to visit me to observe the progress we'd made regarding the disruptions to their communication systems. He was quite interested in the prototype we'd created to duplicate the effect for testing. Between you and me, I believe he was rather taken with the idea of being able to vanish from the network at will, having been under such scrutiny for so long. Why, of course I allowed him to take the prototype. After all, how could I say no to the man who saved the world?"

As those thoughts concluded, Bryan realized that he was feeling a faint pulse in Jacob Westbrook's wrists. He stopped, considering whether the man might still be conscious and whether he should take the time to smother him and definitively end his reign before proceeding, just to be safe.

At that moment, the door to the conference room opened behind him and Bryan Davenport's blood ran cold, knowing there was only one person with the authority to override the biometric lock he'd applied to it.

"You son of a bitch!" Muriel Westbrook exclaimed as she entered the room. "What have you done?"

Immediately, Bryan stood, letting Jacob's arms drop to the floor as he spun around, raising his own hands while he backed away, hoping to lure her to within the dampening device's range. "Muriel! Please! Wait! I can explain!" But the red circle was already forming around his executive rank indicator as Westbrook's ex-wife began to rapidly demote him as quickly as she could.

Davenport managed to stay on his feet through class three and all of class four but when the indicator flipped to a "V," he collapsed onto the ground a few meters away from Jacob and began writhing, clutching the sides of his head and screaming. "No! Please! Don't! I'm sorry!"

Unfazed, Muriel advanced further into the room, continuing the demotion through another four ranks down to the threshold between eight and nine, only stopping when she got close enough to Jacob for her implant to be knocked offline. Seeing that Davenport had been completely immobilized, she turned her attention to the only man she'd ever truly loved and fell to her knees at his side, quickly unfastening the various buttons of his suit jacket, vest, and dress shirt to expose his wounded body.

The hole in Jacob's belly looked serious and she immediately began to apply pressure to it, but the executive was relieved to see that a large medallion he'd been wearing had apparently absorbed most of the shot fired into his chest, the object at its center having been decimated but the deformed slug left visible just under his skin and outside his ribcage as a result.

At her touch, the big man began to stir, lifting his head off the ground with considerable effort. "Muriel!" he croaked out, tears beginning to flow from his eyes.

"I'm here, old friend. You're going to be okay," she assured him. "Do you know what's stopping our implants from working?"

"Jacket pocket. Don't touch the switch," he managed.

Muriel acted quickly, using one of her bloodied hands to carefully retrieve the device before tossing it to a far corner of the room as she maintained pressure on Jacob's more-serious wound.

For a time, panic began to set in as her implant remained offline but finally, after a few seconds of pure anguish, the connection was reestablished. Knowing that Jacob's implant would automatically summon medical assistance for him now that it was able to do so, she turned her attention back to Davenport, intending to demote him to death for what he'd done as he lay drooling on the floor nearby in an effectively-catatonic state.

As if reading her mind, Jacob reached up and put a hand on her shoulder. "Don't, dear. He's not worth it."

For a moment, Muriel set her jaw, seeming determined to act on her impulse regardless of the consequences, then simply said, "Mr. Davenport, you're fired."

Instantly, the "VIII" indicator projected by Bryan's lapel pin exploded in a swarm of disintegrating pixels when he was completely removed from the executive class as a result of being terminated from a position at a rank higher than twelve. He would never again be allowed to hold any executive rank, assuming that he ever recovered from the trauma of his massive demotion, and would live out the rest of his life as an ordinary citizen with a criminal record.

"Indeed," Muriel concluded internally, "a fate worse than death for a man of that sort." She knew Jacob's intention had been more about sparing her than punishing him but she couldn't help acknowledging and appreciating how he'd once again found the best solution for the situation, even in his gravely-injured state.

With that, Muriel watched as a security team entered the room and drug away Bryan Davenport's limp, gasping body, having no doubt been automatically ordered to remove him from the premises as quickly as possible to await one of the city's medical transport pods on the cold, hard ground outside it as any other similarly-terminated executive would. She briefly wondered if any of the angrier members of the crowd surrounding the building might take their frustrations out on him but quickly concluded that any such actions would be a simple case of karmic retribution as far as she was concerned and promptly returned her full attention to Jacob.

First and foremost, she used her implant to ensure that any and all resources of the Pryce Foundation, including nanites if necessary, would be pressed into service to restore him to perfect health as quickly as possible. Muriel then began selecting a new outfit for her old friend to replace the one that had been bloodied, even as she continued to comfort and reassure him while they waited for help to arrive.

CHAPTER 20

EXECUTIVE AUTHORITY

Meanwhile, aboard the Apex, Tom continued to stand awestruck as the executive before him began to address the room.

"You all know who I am," he said simply, "but for the purposes of expediency, you may simply refer to me as Al, or sir if you prefer the formal, for the duration of this mission." He then looked to Pryce, who was still holding his head, clearly not having fully recovered from their ordeal, but just as clearly paying strict attention to the executive and his words. "Note, Mr. Pryce, that I have been temporarily commissioned by the Air Force as a general to eliminate the possibility of any confusion or ambiguity regarding the chain of command aboard this vessel. Is that understood?"

For a moment, the big man's lapel indicator expanded to reveal a single, gold star denoting an official, military rank.

"Yes, sir," the younger man said, using his other hand to offer a proper if somewhat imperfect salute.

"At ease, major," the general said, then addressed the room again, continuing his remarks. "I had hoped that my active participation here would not be required until the mission's final stage but given the loss of communication with Earth, I will assume Mr. Westbrook's role to ensure its success. For the most part, I intend to allow you to continue to operate autonomously as you have to this point; however, I reserve the right to issue orders to any of you at any time and those orders will be carried out without delay or hesitation for nothing less than the sake of humanity's survival. Is that understood?"

To a person, everyone present, including Tom Hallett, immediately responded. "Yes, sir!"

"Excellent," the executive said with a nod. "Proceed."

With that, the crew returned to their stations, Clay intercepting Pryce and leading him to the medical bay as he continued to hold his head but managed to make his own way there without assistance.

Soon, Tom found himself the only one left in the executive's presence, not having a specific post to report to and admittedly well beyond eager to interact with him given the opportunity.

The big man smiled and nodded at the archivist, seeming to read his mind. "Greetings, Mr. Hallett. I'm very pleased to meet you."

"Thank you, sir," Tom said, stepping forward and extending a hand, a bit surprised by his own sense of confidence. "It's a true honor, sir."

Hallett realized, even as the executive took his hand and gave it a firm shake, simply saying "Likewise, sir." in response, that he never would have had the nerve or will to do such a thing if not for his friendship with Jacob and the various interactions they'd had. Indeed, he rapidly concluded that those had been the only things that could have possibly prepared him for such an event.

"Is there anything I can do to help you, sir?" The archivist asked this with his customary sincerity, allowing his hand to linger in the older man's potent grip for a moment longer before relaxing his own hand to indicate that he was ready and willing to complete the gesture.

The executive released Tom's hand after giving it a little, additional squeeze, then replied. "I will have some instructions for you later, Mr. Hallett. Please remain in my presence for the duration of the mission."

Tom nodded immediately.

"For now," the big man continued, "is there anything you would ask of me before we join Dr. Maxwell in the science lab?"

The archivist pondered, struggling to select from the multitude of possible queries he'd accumulated that he knew the man before him was uniquely qualified to answer, then settled on the simplest, most obvious one, knowing it was the question that would trouble him most if it were never addressed. "Why me, sir?"

The executive grinned. "That would take quite a while to explain, Mr. Hallett, and sadly, we lack the time to do so properly." The big man set his jaw, seeming to similarly ponder himself before continuing. "Perhaps it suffices to say that you remind me of myself, particularly when observing your interactions with Mr. Westbrook. When I saw the two of you together, I simply knew that all of this was meant to be."

Tom nodded, not fully comprehending his words but eager to accept the older man's endorsement of his association with Jacob. "I feel the same," he said simply.

Again, the executive nodded. "Shall we proceed then, Mr. Hallett?"

"Yes, sir," Tom said confidently, the other questions melting away in his mind amid a warm, soothing sense of reassurance unlike anything he'd ever experienced. Thus, he dutifully followed the big man to the science lab, almost hypnotized by the methodical sounds of the executive's shoes as they repeatedly made potent, metronome-like contact with the ship's deck plates.

CHAPTER 21

EXECUTIVE DECISIONS

Upon entering the science lab, Tom Hallett and Al found Monique carefully studying one of its main displays, a worried expression on her face.

"Have you completed your analysis, Dr. Maxwell?" The big man asked the question, seemingly not expecting a positive response but more as a matter of formality and a means to initiate the conversation.

The scientist shook her head. "As I feared, sir, I could well spend the rest of my life analyzing this data and not truly understand what's happening here, much less conceive of a way to stop it."

To Tom's surprise, the executive simply nodded and spoke as if she'd given him precisely the answer he'd expected to hear. "It's okay, Monique. I'd hoped for a miracle but never expected one. We will proceed as planned."

"Yes, sir," she said somberly.

"For what it's worth," the big man added, "I know that you of all people will find the answers eventually and I will gladly act to ensure that you're given the time and opportunity to do so."

"Thank you, sir," Maxwell said, not quite managing to look at him as she wiped a tear from her right eye before it could escape and made an obvious effort to maintain her composure.

With that, Al walked over to the room's closest comm panel and activated it, transmitting a message throughout the ship. "All hands, report to the science lab immediately. I have an announcement."

Within a minute, the room was filled with all the active crew members, including Pryce, who the doctor had cleared to continued duty after determining that the damage his brain had suffered wasn't life threatening despite being too severe for the nanites to completely repair it.

Upon gaining their full attention with a simple hand gesture, the big man spoke, allowing his gaze to pass over each of them as he looked around the room. "After consulting with Dr. Maxwell, I have concluded that the best course of action is for the Apex to return to Earth with the data it has accumulated. You will do so immediately after I dismiss you, beginning with a maneuver to reorient the rear of the ship to face the anomaly."

At this, Pryce piped up. "Sir, with respect, we can't just run away. We have to do something!"

Clearly a bit perturbed, the executive directed his attention specifically toward the tactical officer. "I assure you, Adrian, I am going to do something but there is nothing more for the rest of you to do here and there is no point in risking you or the ship any further."

Pryce looked at him incredulously, shaking his head. "What are you talking about, sir? There aren't any weapon systems or deployables at the rear of the ship. There's just the main engines... and an airlock."

"I'm well aware of that, Mr. Pryce. Now, all of you, proceed as instructed. Dismissed!"

With that, the big man began to walk out of the room and Sophia approached a console, executing a command that initiated the ship's gradual, reorientation maneuver as the rest of the crew began to slowly disperse apart from Pryce, who simply stood, shaking his head.

The soldier finally stopped, noting that the executive had turned toward the rear of the ship upon exiting the lab. All at once, a realization clicked in his mind and he rushed to follow him, shoving his way past Tom Hallett and grabbing one of the nanite guns from the rack next to the door as he surged into the long corridor, turning its dial to the red position.

"Hold it right there!" Pryce yelled, readying the rifle and pointing it at the executive, who only paused for a moment before continuing at his original pace toward the engineering section at the rear of the ship. "Stop, or I swear I'll shoot you in the back, you goddamned coward!"

At this, the big man stopped and turned around, a furious expression manifesting on his face. "What, exactly, do you think you're doing, major?"

"I... I don't know... but I know what you're about to do and I sure as hell am not gonna let you do it! You have to come back, face the music, and wait to die just like the rest of us, you selfish bastard!"

Again, the executive's face morphed, this time into an expression of wounded disbelief. "Adrian," he began, making a clear effort to calm himself. "Do you really believe I would do that? That I would throw my life away for no purpose, just to avoid my share of suffering?"

Pryce shook his head slightly but kept the rifle at the ready. "But... there's nothing you could do," he said, his voice quivering. "You're just a fat guy in a fancy suit, no matter what my father says." Behind him, the rest of the crew had gathered in the hall, Tom Hallett quietly moving toward the soldier until he snarled over his shoulder, tightening his grip on the weapon. "Stay back, all of you!"

"Adrian," Sophia said calmly. "There are things you don't know about what's happening here. Things we don't have time to explain."

"Indeed," the big man confirmed, unfastening the button of his suit jacket and opening it before unclipping his tie and flipping it over his shoulder. He then released several of the buttons on his dress shirt and pulled it open to reveal his belly. "If you truly believe that about me, Adrian, then shoot me right here," he said, poking the center of his gut. "After all, if I am what you say I am, and a coward to boot, then that's exactly what I deserve. Isn't that right, Mr. Pryce?"

For a moment, there was a still, silent calm, then Adrian simply said, "Yes, sir," as he aimed and pulled the trigger.

"No!" Tom screamed, watching the red ball of nanites travel through the center of the ship's corridor and strike the executive in the gut in an overwhelmingly-disturbing variation of the events from his nightmare.

For an instant, the mass expanded, creating a bloody crater in the big man's midsection, but it quickly stopped, revealing a metallic surface beneath the layers of flesh, fat and muscle as he fell to one knee and let out a howl of pain, his face wrinkling into an intense grimace and his arms shooting out at his sides in an effort to steady himself.

Immediately, most of the rest of the crew descended on Pryce, tackling him to the ground and pulling the rifle out of his hands to send it sailing toward the front of the ship after Briggs delivered several forceful blows to his head to daze him.

"You crazy son of a bitch!" the engineer exclaimed, continuing to pummel Pryce until the major lost consciousness and Rashid and Mikaela pulled him away, the three of them staring in disbelief at the big man, who finally collapsed to the ground on his back, clearly overwhelmed by the pain he was experiencing but just as clearly still alive as his extremities began to involuntarily squirm.

"That's not possible," Rashid said, shaking his head as he walked away in disbelief. "No one could survive that!"

"Listen up, everybody!" Sophia ordered, obviously attempting to stabilize the situation. "I need you all to stay calm and focus on our task. We still have a mission to complete!"

For the most part, the rest of the crew appeared willing and able to do so, turning their attention to Fields as Tom began to slowly walk toward the fallen executive, who seemed to be gradually recovering on the ground in front of him despite the significant hole in his abdomen. Behind him, the archivist heard the sound of Rashid laughing as the technician picked up the rifle that had been discarded and he instantly knew what was about to happen.

"Rashid, don't," the archivist said, turning to face him as the tech raised the weapon and pointed it vaguely toward the executive, who slowly rose up off the ground, still struggling to get back on his feet.

"He's not even human," the older man said, shaking his head. "Steve died for him and he's not even real!"

"Steve died for all of us," Tom argued, putting up his hands and stepping into Rashid's line of fire, "and whatever he is, Al's about to do the same if you let him." From the moment he'd seen the big man's interaction with Monique Maxwell, the archivist had known that was true and everything he'd seen since had only made the situation and his role in it more clear. He was there to save the executive, just as he'd saved Jacob, to allow him to complete his task, whatever the cost.

"How can you know that?" Rashid asked. "How can we trust... that?" He twitched the gun, gesturing toward the big man, who'd finally managed to right himself, huffing and puffing as he began buttoning his shirt to cover the hole in his belly.

Hallett paused for a moment, knowing that he could never explain his instinct in a way the tech would find plausible or compelling, then realized he wouldn't have to if the others followed suit, shooting a look to Sophia before saying, "If you can't trust him, then trust me."

Again, Rashid shook his head. "No offense, Tom, but I barely know you."

As he'd known she would, Sophia stepped in front of Hallett, raising her own hands and further obscuring the big man behind them. "Then trust me, Rashid."

At this, the tech's resolve seemed to waver but he held his ground until, one by one, each of the remaining crew members took up similar, defensive positions, forming a line that ended with Mikaela standing just a couple meters in front of him when she quietly repeated, "Then trust me, friend."

With that, Rashid deactivated the rifle and let it drop to the floor as tears began to flow from his eyes. "I'm sorry, everyone," he said softly. "What do you want me to do?"

CHAPTER 22

THE LONG GOODBYE

As the Apex hurtled toward the anomaly, rapidly approaching the point of no return, Rashid helped to secure Adrian Pryce in his gravity couch, ensuring that the soldier wouldn't regain consciousness until they returned to Earth. He then made his way to the bridge, taking up a position at the tactical station to complete the orders Sophia had given him.

Meanwhile, in engineering, Tom Hallett and Robert Briggs stood with the executive just outside the ship's rear-facing airlock as the big man finished reassembling his suit to cover the red stain forming on his dress shirt from his wound, which had bled shockingly little despite its severity.

"Is that really you, Al?" The engineer asked, studying the man carefully as he finished making himself as presentable as possible.

"I assure you, Mr. Briggs, I am the man you've always known. I give you my word," the executive said sincerely.

"Okay," Bob acknowledged with a sigh, then set his jaw before nodding. "I believe you."

"Thank you, Robert," the big man said somberly. "That means a great deal to me."

"This really is goodbye then?" The engineer asked, seeming to realize it for the first time.

"For now, old friend," the executive replied, giving his shoulder a couple, quick pats and a squeeze. "For now."

With nothing more to say, Briggs turned and walked away, Al's hand falling to his side as the younger man departed, taking his station at the main engineering console.

The executive then turned his attention to Hallett, removing a small, black cylinder from his right-front trouser pocket as he spoke. "I know what I'm about to ask of you will go against your nature, Tom, but I believe my reasons for doing so will become clear to you soon enough."

"What is it, sir?" Hallett asked, as committed as ever to the big man's cause but somehow less enthralled by him than he'd ever imagined possible, still trying to reconcile what he'd seen beneath the man's suit.

"As the mission's archivist, yours will be the official account of what has transpired here. Others may well make their own claims but yours is the voice that will ultimately be heard and accepted in that regard. I therefore ask that you exclude any mention of my presence here from that record and simply say that the Apex delivered a classified, experimental payload to the anomaly, regardless of the outcome."

"What are you, sir?" Tom asked, knowing that he'd likely never get another chance to do so.

"In truth, Mr. Hallett, I've been many things," Al offered, "but for the purposes of your question, I'll simply say that I have tried above all else to be a good man. I know that answer may not satisfy you but at this point, it's the only one I can give."

"Fair enough," Tom agreed. "Okay. I'll do as you've asked. I give you my word."

"Good man," Al said in a way that Hallett immediately recognized, then held the cylinder up to his right eye and clicked a button on its side. After a moment, he handed the device to Hallett. "As a final request, I ask you to deliver this to Mr. Westbrook. He will know what to do with it."

"Yes, sir," the archivist said, pocketing the cylinder after briefly examining it.

The big man nodded, then pressed a button next to the airlock, stepping inside immediately as it opened. He turned, activating a similar switch on the inside of the chamber to close the door as he spoke one final time. "Goodbye, Mr. Hallett. Thank you for everything."

"Goodbye, sir," Tom managed as the door closed between them, leaving the executive visible only through a small, transparent section in the barrier's center.

Without delay, Al began to work a simple set of controls on the inside of the door, causing a thin, opaque membrane of dark, blue nanites to form next to the outer door before it slid open, revealing the scintillating heart of the anomaly beyond the portal as it brightly shimmered despite the filtering effect of the nanites.

The big man stepped back into the center of the chamber, taking a moment to inspect himself as he kept his back to the exit. He paused, removing a handkerchief from a pocket and using it to wipe away a small blemish from the otherwise-pristine upper of his left shoe, then re-pocketed the cloth. At last, he drew in a deep breath and slowly let it out as he reached for a button below the little window.

Instantly, the nanites disappeared and Al was sucked out of the airlock and off his feet with explosive force, rapidly shrinking to an almost imperceivable swirl of flailing limbs before disappearing completely from view.

Tom put his hand against the glass, steadying himself as his knees buckled and he began to sob, squeezing his eyes closed to block out the burning light from the anomaly while the airlock's outer door slid back into place.

Tumbling through space, Al caught glimpses of the Apex when its main engines fired and the distance between them rapidly expanded, reducing the ship to a tiny, pulsing blob of light within seconds as his vision started to fail. Simultaneously, every cell in his body began to resonate, burning in an excruciating manner far beyond any pain he'd ever experienced as his flesh and blood and bones all boiled in the stew of radiation spewing out of the anomaly. He screamed reflexively until the pain receptors in his brain shorted out, leaving him completely numb but oddly conscious in a manner he hadn't expected. Seizing the moment and knowing it would be his last, the big man brought his heels together and kicked off the shoes that had once been worn by Conrad Pryce, which had always been a bit loose on his feet despite his best efforts to fill them, and sent them each flying in a different direction. He smiled, imagining the elegant cap toes reflecting the light of countless stars while they traveled through the cosmos until the end of time. A moment later, the man who had once been Alan Wells died, his chosen purpose served when his suited corpse plunged into the anomaly a few minutes later.

Aboard the Apex, Tom slowly walked toward the bridge in no particular hurry, feeling disconnected and numb despite the ship's quaking in the midst of its overdrive burn. Finally, after several minutes, he reached the end of the long corridor, the doors to the bridge automatically parting before him to reveal the anomaly undulating in its customary fashion on its massive, main display, apparently growing faster than ever.

At that moment, a sort of shockwave erupted along the structure's outer surface, rapidly rippling through the anomaly until it encompassed it completely. Then, a small, dark spot formed at the phenomenon's center, seeming to draw all the surrounding matter and energy into an expanding vortex.

Tom's mouth hung agape, completely awestruck by the display, which was so simultaneously violent and beautiful that he couldn't help but stare despite the terror it instilled in him, wondering if they might be swallowed by the maelstrom despite their rapid acceleration away from it.

At last, the vortex stopped growing as it consumed the surrounding remnants of the anomaly before collapsing in on itself and disappearing completely.

"Hell yeah!" Bob's voice erupted in Tom's head as their implants all came back online, reestablishing their local network.

"Hell yeah, indeed," the archivist thought as he brought a hand up to his mouth and began to cry again, this time with tears of joy.

CHAPTER 23

THE RETURN

It took a little over a week for the Apex to return to Earth, its supply of nanites having been almost completely exhausted by that point and the conscious crew members surviving on a small cache of rations that had been heavily shielded within a tiny, emergency compartment in the crew quarters.

To conserve resources, Adrian Pryce was kept in stasis within his gravity couch, akin to the backup crew members who hadn't been activated during the mission, until a stable orbit of the planet was achieved.

It had taken a bit of convincing by the rest of the crew, and no small effort on Tom's part, to persuade the soldier to go along with the version of events the archivist had committed to his journal with his heirloom pen, but Pryce eventually came around. Ultimately, he was forced to acknowledge that, whatever Al had been, he had certainly been no coward, and had obviously acted in all of their best interests, making his request one worth honoring. He furthermore, if begrudgingly, apologized to everyone involved for his actions, even burying the hatchet with Robert Briggs by the time the small armada of automated crew modules arrived to retrieve them.

To Tom's great relief, they safely returned to a world that all at once appeared smaller and more fragile than he'd ever considered it to be, despite having been spared from annihilation. As he made his way through the expected but still nearly overwhelming events of their arrival, the archivist did his best to note the details of those experiences for inclusion in his eventual report while ensuring that the magnitude and significance of that poignant realization wouldn't be lost amid them.

After what seemed to him like far too long a wait, Tom Hallett found himself sitting alone in a room on the 33rd floor of the building he'd come to think of as home, impatiently awaiting the arrival of his friend, Jacob Westbrook.

Finally, the room's door opened and the big man walked in, a broad grin on his face. "Lovely to see you again, Tom," he said spreading his arms as the younger man rushed toward him and gave him a big, firm hug.

"Muriel told me what happened," Hallett erupted, giving the executive a little, extra squeeze before stepping back and looking him over more carefully as his eyes began to water. "Are you really okay, Jacob?"

"I am, friend," he said simply, grabbing the archivist's shoulders and looking him over in a similar fashion. "I promise."

Relieved, Hallett smiled, even as he admitted, "I was so worried that I'd made the wrong choice to go. Then, when I heard what that bastard did to you... what he tried to do to you..."

Westbrook shook his head but continued to smile. "It's okay, Tom. You were exactly where you were supposed to be. I assure you."

The archivist took in a deep breath and let it out in a potent, cathartic sigh. "Thank you, Jacob," he said sincerely.

"Any time, buddy," the older man replied, giving Hallett's shoulders a couple, little pats before letting his hands drop to his sides. "Now, do you by chance have something for me?" Westbrook asked this seemingly as a matter of formality, apparently knowing the answer.

Tom nodded, retrieving the black cylinder from his pocket and handing it to the executive.

"Excellent," the big man said, decisively gripping the device in his hand. "Wait right there," he continued. "I have someone here you'll want to meet."

With that, Jacob retreated into the hallway outside the room but quickly returned, pushing a wheelchair containing a large, unconscious, suited gentleman.

Even with his head limp and lowered, Tom immediately recognized the man as Albert Nodwell, the very same class one executive he'd seen sucked out of the Apex's rear airlock a week prior.

"What the hell..." Hallett began but stopped as Jacob put a hand under Nodwell's chin and lifted it until his head was tilted back, noting that Al in fact appeared more dead than unconscious, showing no sign that he was even breathing. Westbrook then used that same hand to pry open the old man's right eyelid and aimed the cylinder's end at the revealed orb with the other, clicking its button.

A few moments later, the big man drew in a deep breath as his body sprang to life, his wingtip-clad feet kicking off the wheelchair's footrests and beginning to squirm as he instinctively brought his hands up toward Westbrook's arms. "Jacob!" He exclaimed. "Is that you?"

"Yes, sir," Westbrook said, lowering his hands and studying his boss's face as it rapidly shifted through various expressions indicating a range of emotions while he huffed and puffed heavily, seemingly trying to catch his breath.

"Unbelievable," Tom said, his mind completely staggered by what he was witnessing.

At the sound of Tom's voice, Nodwell lowered his head and looked directly at the younger man. "Thank you again, Mr. Hallett. Well done!"

For a moment, the archivist's mouth hung open in total disbelief until he finally managed to speak. "Is that really you, Al?"

"It is now," the big man confirmed, "thanks to you," his lapel pin illuminating to reveal his class one executive status as his implant came online.

AUTHOR'S NOTE

When I began my journey as an author, I opted to be a bit conservative with the "Author's Note" in my first novel, "The Big Men," admittedly not being sure if my first book would be my last.

Now, as I sit writing this note, my sixth of its kind in just a few years (counting the ones I did when "Academic Displacement" was released as a standalone novelette and when "Mr. Perkins Goes to Hell" was released via Kindle Vella,) I can't help feeling that I have truly arrived as an author.

At this point, hundreds of people all over the world have read at least one of the books I've written and published, and that audience seems to continue to grow almost daily. I mention this only to properly and humbly acknowledge and appreciate that fact, knowing that so many talented and worthy writers never achieve such success, meager as it may be by comparison to that of others.

In a lot of ways "The Nemesis Effect" represents a very important milestone for me, another vital piece to the literary puzzle I've been assembling via the books I've released and plan to release in the future, which directly and indirectly relate to one another despite being specifically crafted as standalone experiences.

In a manner that fans of those other works will no doubt find simultaneously compelling and vexing, it answers, or at least addresses, many potential questions even as it may well provoke others. In some ways, it it is very direct and literal. In others, it remains purposefully mysterious, subtle, and nuanced. Rest assured that this is all by design and very intentional, and will continue to be the case as I work to complete this project via my next three books over the next few years. That said, "The Nemesis Effect" can and should be seen as a sort of turning point, where the focus of the overall project begins to shift away from introducing broad, new concepts and narrative elements and toward an eventual resolution that will ideally bring a sense of closure and completion for all concerned.

As always, I greatly appreciate your support and acknowledgement of my efforts as an author and sincerely hope that you've enjoyed your time with this book. Moreover, I'd like to specifically thank all my beta readers for the invaluable feedback they provided during its completion. You folks are the best!

Made in the USA
Middletown, DE
28 April 2022

64912539R00066